"Are You Trying To Seduce Me, Brandon?"

He smiled, pleased, as always, with her directness. He would be just as direct. "Yes."

The music had started again, and Veronique followed Brandon's lead. "Overconfidence leads to mistakes," she teased.

"I know what I want, and I'm going after it."

"I'm not going to make it easy for you," Veronique warned, not even blinking at the lie. She was such a fraud—she was his already.

"Oh? What will I have to do? This..." He pressed his lips to her ear, then caught the sensitive lobe between his teeth and nipped. "Or this..." He trailed his lips down the side of her throat, pausing now and again to taste with the tip of his tongue. "Or maybe this..." His lips caught hers in a long, thorough kiss.

When he lifted his head he whispered, "Well, Veronique?"

Dear Reader:

It takes two to tango, and we've declared 1989 the "Year of the Man" at Silhouette Desire. We're honoring that perfect partner, the magnificent male, the one without whom there would be no romance. From January to December, 1989 will be a twelve-month extravaganza, spotlighting one book each month as a tribute to the Silhouette Desire hero—our *Man-of-the-Month*!

You'll find these men created by your favorite authors utterly irresistible. March, traditionally the month that "comes in like a lion and goes out like a lamb," brings a hero to match in Jennifer Greene's Mr. March, and Naomi Horton's Slater McCall is indeed a *Dangerous Kind of Man*, coming in April.

Don't let these men get away!

Yours,

Isabel Swift
Senior Editor & Editorial Coordinator

ERICA SPINDLER
Chances Are

Silhouette Desire

Published by Silhouette Books New York

America's Publisher of Contemporary Romance

SILHOUETTE BOOKS
300 East 42nd St., New York, N.Y. 10017

ISBN: 0-373-05482-3

First Silhouette Books printing March 1989

Books by Erica Spindler

Silhouette Desire

Heaven Sent #442
Chances Are #482

ERICA SPINDLER

came to writing from the visual arts and has numerous one-person, invitational and group exhibitions to her credit. She still teaches art classes in addition to her writing. "It seems only natural to me that I should be writing romance," says Erica. "My paintings had the same spirit of optimism and romanticism that my stories do."

A descendant of Marie Duplessis, the most famous courtesan of her day and the inspiration for Dumas's *Camille*, Erica lives with her husband in New Orleans, where she does most of her writing in a penthouse that affords a panoramic view of that intriguing, history-rich city.

Mom,
for your strength and courage,
for your unconditional love,
for showing me a woman
can be anything she wants to be,
this and all my successes are for you.

Prologue

The graveside was quiet, the stillness broken only by the priest's murmured eulogy and the occasional sound of a passing car. The aboveground tombs caught the noonday sun, and long, stark shadows were cast on the manicured grass and neatly tended walkways.

A tall wrought-iron fence circled the small cemetery in the heart of the New Orleans Garden District. Lining the fence were azalea bushes in full bloom; the profusion of magenta and pink flowers was an affirmation of life in a place reserved for death.

The old man stood just outside the cemetery gate. His complexion was pasty, and his hand shook as he reached up to push away the thatch of still-thick silver hair that fell across his forehead. He looked down at his light blue suit, one corner of his mouth lifting in wry amusement—it figured, his wife had always liked this suit better than he had.

With a heavy sigh, he pushed open the gate and walked through, remembering too late that he didn't have to worry about opening doors or gates anymore. He approached the group gathered around the casket, stopping only when he was close enough to see their faces. Everyone was there, respectfully outfitted in both garb and expression. He supposed he should be honored that so many had come for him today, but it was difficult to feel appreciated when the society editor from the *Times Picayune* was also in attendance and taking notes.

The old man's watery-blue eyes regarded the mourners. There were three people here today whose lives were about to change drastically. If they didn't, he was lost.

Almost unwittingly his gaze went to a wizened man with eyes as sharp and clear as a twenty-year-old's. Jerome Delacroix was ruthless and a tyrant. The old man's shoulders slumped as he wished he could have seen in life what he saw in death.

Regrets. He'd done some pretty nasty things in his life. He'd been given one last chance to make them right. Lifting his eyes heavenward, he wished for a cigar, then reminded himself that he was supposed to be mending his ways—all of them

One

Veronique Delacroix wore dime-store sunglasses with zebra-striped frames; her boots, like her jeans, were red. Her one concession to propriety was a black suede jacket made of the softest kid. She shoved her hands into its pockets and stared at the four black limousines in front of the Rhodes mansion. She hated these society gatherings and usually avoided them like the plague. But her mother had asked for her company, so here she was.

The wind pulled at and lifted her long silk scarf, and as she looked from the cars to her mother, it fluttered behind her. She held out her arm. "Ready, Maman?" she asked, using the French pronunciation. Her mother nodded and took her arm. Together they headed up the curving brick walk.

"I wish your grandfather would have come," Marie said, her brow wrinkling with concern. "He and Blake were friends. The family will expect to see him and..." Her words trailed off, and she took a deep breath. "It doesn't seem right, that's all."

Veronique swallowed the choice words that sprang to her tongue about her grandfather Jerome and squeezed her mother's arm. "You know how he is," she murmured instead as they approached the awesome house. Built in the late 1800s, it reflected the eclectic revival style of Victoria's reign, complete with gingerbread, a turret and portico. This house, like many others up and down St. Charles Avenue, was fitted with leaded glass windows. One of her earliest memories was of riding the streetcar down the Avenue at night with her mother and being entranced by the light flooding through the faceted glass.

The butler opened the door before Veronique had a chance to knock. He escorted them through the huge foyer and into the main parlor. When she caught sight of Lily St. Germaine heading their way, Veronique muttered a short, stern word under her breath. The woman was a gossip and a snob. The biggest of both. In fact, Veronique was sure several of the stories that had circulated over the years about "that Veronique Delacroix" had come right from this particular horse's mouth.

This could be fun, Veronique decided. Lily St. Germaine would never pass up such a golden opportunity to snub her. A gambler by nature, Veronique eyed the woman's expression—the light in her eyes, the tilt of her lips, and determined gait. *A hot-fudge sundae says she'll insult me within two minutes of arrival; if not, I'll eat something nutritious for dinner.* Veronique glanced at her watch the moment Lily stopped in front of them, an overbright smile on her lips.

"Marie, your dress is lovely. And just your color, too," the woman gushed. "I've never seen you look better."

Veronique waited, silently counting down from ten. When she reached five, Mrs. St. Germaine turned suddenly. Slowly, the large woman lowered her gaze, sweeping Veronique from head to toe. She arched one meticulously penciled eyebrow in distaste, then purposefully turned her back to her.

Veronique's lips curved—one minute, twelve seconds. There was a hot-fudge sundae in her future, thanks to an oh-so-predictable snob.

"So, Marie, how are you dear? You look marvelous. I *do* so hope that you and I..."

And a fake, Veronique thought. From her fabricated concern to her dramatic gestures, the woman was as phony as pink plastic flamingos. Veronique had never been able to take plastic birds seriously.

Veronique touched her mother's elbow. "Excuse me. I'm going to the bar. Would you care for anything?"

"No, thank you. Run along, sweetie."

"Run along, sweetie?" Veronique caught her bottom lip to keep from laughing. "Oh, Maman," she murmured, giving her a quick kiss on the cheek. "You're something else." Her eyes shifted to Lily's disapproving face. She winked, and the woman looked obviously appalled. "You're something else, too, Mrs. St. Germaine."

Laughing to her herself, she turned toward the bar. As she wormed her way around and through the mourners, she caught snatches of conversation.

"...I told him to stop working so hard. If he'd listened to me..."

Self-important. She edged by another clique of women.

"...The poor thing, a widow at her age! And Brandon...they were so close..."

Affected. Veronique continued moving through the room.

"...He's the only heir. The estate must be incredible. I'd love to get a peek at..."

Veronique shook her head, wondering if anyone was here to pay their respects. It seemed they were more interested in gossip and their own aggrandizement. As well as being seen, she thought, catching sight of Sissy Dunbar, the society editor for the *Times Picayune*. At least she'd left her photographer behind.

"Drink, miss?"

The bartender was an ancient black man with bright white hair. "Yes." Veronique smiled. "Whiskey, neat."

While he poured her drink, she glanced back at her mother. Several other women had joined her, and they were in the middle of an avid discussion. One corner of her mobile mouth lifted as Mrs. St. Germaine gestured grandly and her mother's eyes widened in shock. They were undoubtedly barbecuing some innocent bystander.

"Here you are, miss."

"Thanks." Veronique took the glass and sipped. She held the heady liquor on her tongue for a moment before swallowing. Whiskey was a tough drink, gutsy and decisive. That's why she liked it.

Her gaze moved back to her mother and softened. There were advantages to being the black sheep. The biggest was that everyone was so scandalized by her presence and behavior, they'd forgotten her mother's sin and had accepted her back into their elite circle.

And that meant the world to her mother. These people were Marie's friends. She'd grown up with them. She understood them, and they her. Veronique remembered how alone and sad her mother had been—ostracized by her friends, shunned by her family. Veronique tightened her fingers around the glass. And all because of one very human mistake.

A strange prickling sensation ran up her spine, and she took her gaze from her mother, only to meet the curious eyes of Sissy Dunbar. Rats. She and the society editor had tangled before, and she had no desire to repeat the performance. Veronique smiled and held up her drink in greeting, then ducked through the open doors that led out onto the gallery. She sucked in a deep breath and began walking.

Sissy was tenacious and Veronique had no doubt that if she wanted to talk to her, she would follow.

The gallery ran the full length of the house and was lined with French doors that led to various rooms on the first floor. She peeked through the first open door she came to, making a small sound of pleasure as she glimpsed an ornate old pool table. Thinking the room empty, she slipped inside.

Alone in the billiard room, Brandon stood ramrod straight as he stared out the veranda doors at the garden. His shoulders and neck ached from tension; his head throbbed from a combination of bottled emotions and squinting against the light. But worse, there was a hollowness inside him. It had been there since his father's death. It was an emptiness that hadn't gone away with food or drink. He understood it—the void had come with the knowledge that there were no more chances, that time had run out.

Brandon looked down at his hands, then turned away from the brilliant spring garden. He and his father had been connected by flesh and blood, yet they hadn't known each other—not in the way a father and son should. They'd never gone to a ball game together or fishing. Nor could he remember a heart-to-heart talk or a shared joke. They'd merely existed in their connected space.

Brandon crossed to the cue racks. His father had been busy building a retailing empire. Brandon acknowledged a surge of pride for the man who'd founded Rhodes at an age just shy of thirty and who'd been the driving force behind its success. If he hadn't had the time or energy to get to know his son or been generous enough to share himself or his success, well, perhaps that was part of being the best.

Brandon flexed his fingers in frustration. If only it hadn't been so sudden, if only he'd hung on a little longer...maybe they would have made the effort and touched each other. He shook his head and sighed. It was over.

There was a breathy exclamation behind him, and Brandon turned. A woman wearing red jeans and a black suede jacket stood in the doorway. The jeans fit like a second skin, outlining a figure that was almost boyishly thin. Her hair was thick, straight and the exact shade of the liquor in her glass. At the cemetery he'd seen a flash of red from the corner of his eye and had thought himself mistaken. As she took a step toward the center of the room, resentment both at the intrusion and her choice of dress washed over him. "May I help you?"

Veronique's gaze flew to his in surprise. "Excuse me! I didn't know you were here. I thought—"

"You thought you'd take the opportunity for an unguided tour?" he supplied. "Or have you just lost your way? The *mourners* are all in the main parlor."

"I'll go now." She swung around to leave, then stopped and turned back toward him. His face was etched with grief, his eyes dark with pain. She couldn't leave without saying something, without somehow trying to ease his suffering. "I'm really sorry, you know."

This time her exit was stopped by Brandon. "No, I don't know," he returned coldly. "Are you 'really sorry'? If so, you're one of the few people here who is."

She tipped her chin. "I wouldn't have said it if I hadn't meant it."

"Oh? I can see how grief-stricken you are." His eyes raked over her. "Is red the newest trend in funeral wear?"

Veronique's spine stiffened. "What I wear is a statement about who I am, not how I feel or my sincerity."

Brandon emitted a short bark of laughter. "Maybe you're right—everyone else looks as if the world has come to an end." He crossed to the pool table and picked up the cue ball. He stared at the smooth white ball for long moments. Almost to himself, he said, "Someone asked me if I felt more powerful, now that I'm the president of Rhodes. As if that had even crossed my mind."

For a second Veronique thought he was going to throw the ball. Instead, he carefully put it down and turned away from her. It was an obvious bid for her to get lost, but he seemed so alone, so in need of comfort, that she couldn't bring herself to move. Knowing she was intruding, she murmured, "What matters is the way you and your father felt about each other. And the way you feel right now. Not what all those superficial twits in the other room are thinking or saying."

Brandon flinched. Without realizing it, this stranger had touched the very heart of his grief. "You want to hear something funny?" he asked, his voice hard. "I don't know *how* I felt about my father. I don't know if I loved him or hated him."

"Those are both strong emotions," she said quietly, watching as he strode to the French doors and looked out at the lushly landscaped yard. His shoulders were broad and strong; he held himself like a man who understood much about control but little about pain. When he swung back around, Veronique saw that a muscle worked in his jaw.

"I was never allowed to sit at his desk. Not at the store, not in his study here. And now those desks and everything in them are mine. Does that make sense?"

Veronique didn't answer because he didn't expect her to.

"He was a crusty one all right, smart and shrewd. He could be kind, but more often he chose not to be." He dragged a hand through his hair. "I think he loved my mother, or maybe they just existed well together. I'm not even sure of that."

He paused, his eyebrows drawing together in thought. After a moment he looked back at her. "I'm proud of his business achievements. Rhodes is the finest store in the South. For five years running our yearly sales have exceeded that of every other privately-owned retail establishment in the country. We've been written up in *Accents*, *Ultra*

and *Southern Living*, to name a few. Building a business of
that magnitude takes..."

He didn't finish the sentence, but instead crossed to stand
in front of her. Silently, he took the glass from her hands
and tossed back the remainder of the drink. It burned, and
he wished for another. "In truth, I have no idea who Blake
Rhodes was. Now I never will."

Her heart ached for him. She understood the anger that
came with finality. She sympathized with the frustration
that came with the certainty of defeat. "It seems we're in the
same boat, you and I," she murmured, a catch in her voice.

"Oh?"

"I didn't know my father, either." He'd handed the glass
back; she held it to her lips, hoping to catch the last fiery
drop on her tongue.

"How did you manage?" he asked, his eyes searching her
face.

She put the glass aside. "As best I could. I'm still dealing with it, still coping." She pushed the hair away from her
face. "When I said I didn't know who my father was, I
meant that literally."

This was the woman he'd heard so much about, Brandon
realized. This was the legend, Veronique Delacroix. "You're
Marie's daughter."

This time Veronique swung away from him. "Interesting," she murmured, picking up the cue ball, "that you
should instantly know me by my filial status." But it was
easy, she thought. She was the only bastard in the group—
or rather, the only one everyone knew about. The ivory ball
was smooth and cool against her palm. She rolled it across
the table; it bounced off the cushion and rolled back to her.
"Do you play?" she asked suddenly.

He cocked his head. Something had changed—in her
voice, her stance, her eyes. "Of course."

She stuck her hand in her pocket and pulled out a crumpled ten. She laid it on the rail and smiled wickedly.

"Straight pool. First player to one hundred wins." Without waiting for an answer, she crossed to the cue racks mounted on the wall behind her. She selected a cue, tested its weight, balance and length. She chalked the tip, then looked at him, arching her eyebrows in question. "Shall we flip a coin for the break?"

"Oh, ladies first." His lips twitched, and he gestured toward the table. "Please."

"Chivalrous but unwise," Veronique said, racking the balls. "However, if you insist."

Brandon watched as she readied for the break. She held the cue like a pro, loosely but with absolute control. Her eyes were narrowed as she lined up the shot; her arm movement was smooth. He grimaced as the cue ball hit the apex of racked balls with a crack. A perfect break. Four balls dropped into pockets.

"Six, off the side and into the corner."

With a combination of surprise and admiration, Brandon watched as one after another she called the shot and sank the ball. "You've played this game before."

"Once or twice." Her laughing eyes lifted from the table to meet his. She liked having caught him off guard and smiled as she lowered her gaze once again to the table. "Haven't you ever known a woman who could play pool? Eight in the corner pocket."

"Not like this." Brandon shoved his hands in his pockets and rocked back on his heels. "A real hustler, aren't you?"

She sank the last ball, then began to rerack. "Let's just say I've spent a little time in pool halls." She picked up the square of blue chalk and expertly twisted it over the tip. "In fact, I used to sneak into Cooter Brown's before I was eighteen."

"No kidding," he murmured as she executed another flawless break.

"Mmm. Once—four off the side—I was busted for being underage. They dropped the charges because I hadn't had a drink. I didn't sneak in to drink. I went to play."

He cocked his head. "And make money."

Veronique just laughed and called another shot. She sank it neatly.

"So—" Brandon leaned against the table and folded his arms across his chest "—what else did you do before you were eighteen?"

Her eyes lifted to his. "That's a rather loaded question, Mr. Rhodes. Fifteen off the one and into the side." The shot missed its mark by an inch. "Blast," Veronique muttered. "I hate stupid mistakes."

"I wouldn't sneeze at thirty-six to nothing," Brandon said, picking up his cue.

"That doesn't justify stupidity. Besides—" she eyed him, noting the ease with which he held the cue "—I have the feeling to underestimate you would be the biggest mistake of all."

Brandon's lips curved. "You're probably right," he murmured, then sank two balls with one shot.

Veronique watched as he set up his next shot. One corner of her mouth lifted in wry amusement. She'd missed the shot because she'd let him distract her. It hadn't been the saucy question that had blown her concentration—although she had to hand it to him, he was either totally ingenuous or damn clever. It had been his eyes. She'd looked up and lost herself in them. They were the most amazing color—a perfect gray, warm and smoky—and surrounded by sooty lashes.

Veronique tilted her head. But the thing she liked best about his face was his eyebrows. Sweeping and dark, they had a high natural arch that gave him a rakish, dangerous appearance. Would he be as dangerous as he looked? Her pulse fluttered, just a little, at the answer, and she smiled to herself. She'd never been one to run from trouble.

"Good shot," she murmured as he completed a particularly tricky maneuver.

"Thanks." He glanced at her from the corners of his eyes. "Worried?"

"Not unless you're planning to sink the next sixty-four balls." She pulled a small ladder-back chair away from the wall, swung it around and straddled it. "Misjudge one shot and the game's mine. I won't give you another chance."

Brandon propped his cue against the table and slipped out of his dark jacket. "You're pretty cocky." He shot her an amused glance as he rolled up his shirt sleeves.

Veronique shrugged. "I know my capabilities."

"Yeah?" Brandon bent and lined up his shot. He looked back up at her the moment the cue hit the ball. "So do I."

Minutes passed without them speaking. The only sounds in the room were Brandon's murmured calls, the crack of ivory against ivory and the muffled thumps of balls dropping into pockets. Veronique's fingers curled around the slats of the chair as she watched him bend and straighten, then move around the table to make another shot. The fabric of his white shirt strained across his shoulders as he pulled back on the cue, then followed through. A custommade shirt, she assessed, eyeing the breadth of his shoulders and the narrowness of his hips. He must belong to a club, she thought, idly running her fingers through her hair. Her lips tilted. He was the health-club type. She'd tried a gym but found it, well...tiresome.

Her thoughts returned to the game. He'd sunk seventy-two. Blast, he could go all the way. Maybe she would have to— Her speculations were interrupted by the sound of the door to the billiard room opening and a surprised gasp. Veronique's eyes crinkled at the corners. In the doorway stood Lily St. Germain, Sissy Dunbar and a woman Veronique didn't recognize.

"Brandon!" The indignant word flew past the unknown woman's lips.

He pulled up a fraction on the cue, and the three ball, instead of dropping into the pocket, balanced on the very edge. "Damn." Shaking his head, his eyes shifted from the missed shot to the doorway. He straightened slowly. "Yes, Aunt Isabella?"

His aunt released her breath in a short huff. "What are you doing?"

He arched one dark eyebrow, sardonically. "I think that's obvious."

"But you should be..." Her words trailed off at his thunderous expression. She stared at him a moment, then turned and marched from the room. The other two, after tossing accusing glances at Veronique, followed her.

Veronique caught her lower lip to keep from laughing, then stood. "Tough break, you were close." She picked up her cue and chalked the tip, then lined up the shot. "Say good-night, Gracie." The three ball dropped into the pocket.

"Are your ears burning?" Brandon's eyes rested on the curve of her rear as she bent to make a shot. Nice.

"Perpetually."

His gaze trailed down her impossibly long legs then back up, lingering on the place where black suede met red denim. "You don't mind?"

She glanced at him over her shoulder. "Should I?"

Brandon's gaze jerked up to hers as he realized he'd been thinking of tempting curves and alluring hollows when he should have been thinking of his father. "I'm sorry, what?"

She bent to make another shot. "Should I mind people talking about me?"

Brandon cursed under his breath, stood and moved to the other side of the table. "I've never thought about it."

"That means you've always played by the rules." She sank the last ball and began to rerack.

"And you don't?" he asked, folding his arms across his chest.

"I stopped a long time ago." The polished wood slid smoothly between her fingers; three balls dropped into pockets.

"No regrets?"

"I gave up regrets when I gave up rules. It makes life a lot more fun." Her eyes met his. She wouldn't ask him about regrets; right now he was consumed with them. Instead, she smiled. "Kiss your ten bucks goodbye." She took the shot, the ball dropped into the pocket. "Could I interest you in another game? Perhaps double or nothing?"

Brandon wasn't sure whether he was annoyed or amused. "Why do I have the feeling I'm being suckered?"

"Because you're astute," she said, not bothering to hide the laughter in her voice. She slipped the two bills into her pocket and sauntered toward the door. "Enjoyed it, Rhodes. Let's play again sometime."

What a strange woman, Brandon thought as she ducked out the way she'd come in. He crossed to the French doors and watched her progress down the gallery until she disappeared through the parlor door. He'd always thought the stories of her exploits, if not totally fabricated, were embellished. Now he wasn't so sure. Maybe he would have the opportunity to ask her one day.

After long moments of staring out at the yard, Brandon shook his head and turned away from the beautiful day. Tomorrow he would have to begin the transition at Rhodes. It was the last thing he wanted to think about, certainly the last thing he wanted to do, but the store wouldn't maintain for long without a president. First he would have to—

There was a discreet knock at the door before it opened. The obviously flustered butler stepped into the room carrying a bottle of Jack Daniel's and a glass on a tray. "Yes, Winston?"

"Sir, a..." The man cleared his throat. "A young...lady said you required this." He set it on the butler's table. "Will there be anything else?"

"No. Thank you, Winston." Brandon smiled to himself as he poured a drink. Veronique Delacroix was a strange woman with a lot of class.

Two

Morning, Chip," Veronique called out as she entered the display department of Rhodes. She tossed the small white bag that contained her breakfast onto the table and headed for the coffeepot. "Welcome back."

"Why are *you* so cheerful?" her assistant mumbled, looking at her over the top of the sports page. "It's Monday. Or haven't you heard?"

Her laugh was husky. "What a grump. Save me the comics, will you?" After pouring herself a cup of coffee and adding generous amounts of both cream and sugar, she crossed to where Chip sat. She snitched the funnies, then plopped onto a metal folding chair that was dusty and crusted with years of paint splatters. Her gaze wandered over the cluttered room. It never ceased to amaze her that their beautiful, pristine displays were created in this chaos. She smiled. "Artistic ambience. Don't you love it?"

"Not on Monday mornings."

"Fine." Veronique rested her sneakered feet on the worktable in front of her. "No cheese-filled croissants for you." Her lips tilted a moment before Chip's head snapped out from behind the paper.

"Croissants?" He ran a hand through his sandy hair, still rumpled with sleep. His grin was sheepish. "I'll be civil."

"I thought so." She handed him a pastry and a napkin. "Anything exciting happen on your vacation?"

"Our car broke down halfway to Disney World, and Sheila and I are fighting."

Veronique swallowed a laugh along with a bite of croissant. "You two are always fighting. Got any new news, any juicy gossip?"

"I'm sure you heard about Mr. Rhodes."

For a moment the only sound in the room was the crackling of Chip's newspaper. "I was at the funeral," Veronique murmured. She rested her chin on her fist. After a moment, she tipped her head and her eyes met Chip's once again. "What do you know about Brandon Rhodes?"

"Only what I've heard. He's bright—attended Harvard Business School. He's the model of the successful young executive." Chip stood and crossed to the coffeepot. "Rumor is he was dissatisfied with his position as the company's public-relations representative and wanted a hand in the day-to-day running of the store. Why?"

She lowered her eyes and shrugged. "Just wondered, him being the new boss and all." The truth was, she'd thought of him countless times over the last week. And she wasn't sure why.

"Rumor also has it, he and his father weren't close."

"Mmm," she murmured noncommittally. She took the last bite of her croissant, then washed it down with a swallow of coffee. "Ready to get going?"

"As ready as I'll ever be." Chip stood, and together they headed upstairs.

An hour and a half later, Veronique stepped back to eye the display in progress. "Hey, Chip, what do you think?"

"It needs more red," he responded dryly. "Would you hand me the pins."

"Pssst . . . Veronique."

Veronique peered over the side of the platform at one of the salesgirls from cosmetics. She was waving a magazine. "What's up, Deb?"

"You've got to take a look at this." The petite brunette was practically dancing with excitement.

"What is it?"

"Mr. March. Come down now, before the store opens."

"Toss it up to me."

Debbie's expression was horrified. "What if I miss?"

"You won't." Veronique held out her hands, catcher-style.

The salesgirl shrugged. "All right."

Veronique caught the magazine by the very edge of the first page. It was the latest issue of *Pillow Talk*, and staring back at her was a picture of a blond Adonis wearing skin-tight ski pants and a come-hither smile. She flipped it open to the centerfold. "Oh, my."

"Let me see." Chip looked over her shoulder. "That can't be real."

Veronique cocked her head and turned the magazine sideways. "I don't know. It looks authentic to me."

Chip frowned and plucked the magazine from her hands. "This photo's been retouched. I'm sure of it."

"Sour grapes, Chip?" she teased. When he muttered several choice words and handed the magazine back, Veronique laughed and looked over the side of the platform for her friend. She was across the aisle, in the Ralph Lauren shop. "Hey, Debbie . . . catch!" At the same moment she tossed the magazine, Debbie signaled frantically, then ducked behind a rack. Veronique understood too late her friend's bizarre behavior. The magazine landed, centerfold up, at Brandon Rhodes's feet.

"Double damn," she muttered as he paused, then bent over and picked it up. For long moments he stared at the photograph before slowly lifting his eyes to her. Veronique took a deep breath. "I only buy them to read the articles," she called down.

Brandon's lips twitched. "I'll bet."

Veronique balanced on the balls of her feet and rested her elbows on her knees. "No, really. Mr. March didn't interest me a bit."

Brandon rolled up the magazine and thoughtfully slapped it against his palm. "Why didn't you tell me you worked for me?"

Veronique smiled and shrugged. "You never asked."

"For an employee talking to her boss you're pretty—"

"Impertinent," she supplied, liking the way his lips tipped up at the corners. "We all have to be good at something."

Brandon worked to maintain a stern expression despite his desire to laugh. "You and my father must have gotten along great."

"Mmm." Veronique tugged on the end of her braid. "We avoided each other. It worked out quite nicely."

Brandon shook his head. She was crazier than he'd first thought. Weren't all artists supposed to be a little nuts? "I'd like to talk to you about the display department."

She sat, then began swinging her legs over the edge of the platform. "Talk away."

"I hardly think shouting up to you is appropriate." He tossed her the magazine; she caught it neatly. "Why don't you and Mr. March come up to my office when you're finished here?" Without another word, he turned and walked away.

Veronique stood and placed her hands on her hips. "Well, goodbye to you, too."

"Veronique, it would be nice to get those pins today."

She tore her eyes from Brandon Rhodes's stiff back and squared shoulders to glance at Chip. "Yeah, sorry."

"No problem." He stuffed red fabric into a large wicker basket. "Great stunt, by the way."

"Right." Veronique jabbed one of the long pins into the fabric.

"In fact, it should take you a long way to a promotion."

"Smart aleck," Veronique muttered. "Besides, it could have been worse."

"Oh, sure. The magazine could have landed in the perfumes, sent several of the most expensive crashing to the floor and stunk up the store for a week."

"Eat navel lint and die, Carson." Their eyes met, and they laughed in unison.

The pungent odor of cigars hung in the air. Brandon frowned at the empty room. Hand still on the doorknob, he swung back around. "Maggie, who's been in my office this morning?"

Startled, the receptionist's eyes met his. "Why, no one, Mr. Rhodes."

"Impossible. My office reeks of cigars."

The receptionist stood, obviously flustered. "Maybe it's just the leftovers—"

"See for yourself." Brandon moved aside so she could step into the office. Although dissipating, there was a faint haze of smoke and a definite odor.

"I don't understand. I was at my desk all morning. No one could have entered without me seeing them." She pushed her glasses back up the bridge of her nose, a thoughtful expression on her face. "Wait...right before you came in I went down the hall to use the copier. But there wasn't time..." Her words trailed off. "I closed the door behind me," she finally said.

"It's not your fault, Maggie. You were doing your job." Brandon ran a hand through his hair and released his breath

in a frustrated sigh. "From now on lock my office whenever you leave. And call security and notify them." She
nodded and hurried back to her desk.

Brandon shut the office door and strode across the room.
He stopped just short of the desk and looked back at the
door. He felt as if someone were watching him. Shaking his
head, he settled into the leather swivel chair behind the desk.

The chair creaked as he leaned back. He remembered the
sound from everytime his father had sat in this chair. He ran
his hand along the polished tabletop. This desk had seemed
huge when he'd been ten, and his father had always seemed
larger than life behind it.

He looked around the room. Although it was a large office, it seemed cramped because of the massive wine-col-
ored leather-and-mahogany furniture and the years of
business and personal memorabilia that covered the walls
and shelves. Three walls were exposed brick, the fourth was
a picture window. The window looked out over the busiest
street in New Orleans's central business district, Canal
Street, and provided enough light to keep the room from
being gloomy, but not enough to make it cheerful.

Brandon leaned back in the chair, testing its spring and
feeling like an impostor. He had to put aside his father's
death and get to work. There was a lot of it to do. Besides
the everyday business of running an establishment of this
size, Rhodes was in the middle of renovating the Atlanta
store and in the process of determining the profitability of
a new store in Dallas.

In the last two days he'd gone through all his father's papers and had talked to the attorneys and accountants. He
had meetings scheduled for the rest of the week: buyers on
Tuesday, department heads on Wednesday, advertising and
publicity on Friday.

Brandon pulled out the Dallas file. As he did, a key
dropped to the floor. What? he wondered, bending to pick
it up. He turned the small unmarked key over in his hand.

It looked like the key to a safety deposit box. In fact—he pulled out his key ring—it looked exactly like the keys to his father's other two boxes.

But according to the will there were *only* two boxes. He'd gone over everything with his legal staff. There wasn't supposed to be anything else. He reached for the phone to call his mother, then thought better of it. What if the box contained something his father hadn't wanted her to see? Like the remnants of a love affair?

Brandon opened the file and carefully thumbed through the papers. He'd used this file yesterday and there hadn't been a key. But there must have been, he assured himself. It had to have been caught in a fold, or maybe it had been in an unsealed envelope.

His musings were interrupted by the intercom. "Veronique Delacroix is here to see you."

"Send her in, Maggie." Brandon closed the file and tucked the key into his pocket.

Veronique entered the office, glancing around in frank curiosity. "You wanted to see me?"

"Yes. Have a seat." Brandon watched as she crossed the room. She looked ready for the jungle. She wore khaki-colored safari pants, a camouflage-print shirt and a red bandanna. All that was missing was a pith helmet. He smiled to himself. He could picture her in the jungle all right—conquering it.

"What's up?" She settled into the chair across from him.

He pulled out a file and flipped it open. What was that perfume she was wearing? She smelled like a field of wild-flowers. "You've been with us for five years," Brandon said, his crisp tone belying his thoughts.

"Yes."

"You have an art degree from the University of New Orleans."

"Yes." Veronique shifted in her seat. He was barking out her statistics like a drill sergeant.

"You were promoted to head of the Canal Street display department eighteen months ago."

"Yes." Her eyes swept over him, then crinkled at the corners. He obviously wanted their dealings to be strictly business. Well, there was nothing she liked better than crossing boundary lines. "Brandon?"

He lifted his gaze from the file to meet hers. "Yes?"

"How are you?" she asked softly.

He stared at her for a moment, then murmured, "Over the worst of it."

"I'm glad."

Several seconds ticked by before Brandon realized he was still staring at her. When he did, he silently swore and looked back down at the file in front of him. "Now, about your department. Overall I'm pleased with your performance. However, there are some problems. The main windows, mannequins and the large displays like the one you were working on this morning look terrific."

She knew what was coming. She beat him to it. "But the counter and fixture-top displays are a mess."

"Exactly." Brandon leaned back in his chair. "As are the departmental mannequins and minor windows along the side entrances. They look as if they were thrown together or done by the salespeople."

Veronique sighed and stood up. She walked to the picture window and looked out at Canal Street. After a moment, she turned back to him. "I'm aware of every aspect of this store's look. I cringe when I see some of the sloppy, mishmash arrangements that are passing for displays." She toyed with the end of her braid. "And yes, some of them *are* put together by the salespeople."

"Yet you let it continue."

Veronique's spine stiffened, and she shot him an annoyed glance. It really was a shame he was so damn handsome. "If you'd done your homework—" she gestured toward the file "—you'd know that your father cut the display budget every year for the last three. We've gone from six full-time artists, to four, to two. Chip and I are barely keeping up. We make sure the areas that are most visible are done well. There's been no money for new props or fixtures, and the old ones—'' she held her hands out, palms up ''—are beginning to look old.''

"You sound frustrated," he murmured.

"I *am* frustrated. I hate to see the look of the store going downhill. And I hate being associated with sloppy work."

"Yet you haven't quit. From what I've seen, you're good. Why haven't you looked elsewhere?"

She slipped her hands into her pockets, her expression thoughtful. "Because, despite your father's insanity, this is a great store to work for. The other day you called this the finest store in the South, and you were right. I could move over to Macy's or Saks, but there the display department would always be a stepchild to the New York and Los Angeles display areas.'' She turned and pinned him with a direct look. "What's all this leading to?"

The room was quiet but for the creaking of the chair as Brandon leaned forward. He admired her forthright approach and appreciated her honesty. "I'd like your opinion of the display department—where you think it should go and what you think needs changing."

"All right." Veronique nodded, not bothering to conceal her excitement. She'd waited a long time for the chance to present her ideas and for the possibility to put her mark on this store. "I'm going to be honest. We look dated. Five years ago we looked good—lush, rich, elegant. But in five years our buying public has become visually more sophisticated. Like the addict who keeps looking for a better high, the public needs something new, something different to get their attention. In five years we've gone from elegant to stodgy, lush to slightly shabby."

Brandon toyed with a pencil. "What do you suggest?"

"Rock 'n' roll," Veronique said crisply. His eyes met hers, and he arched his eyebrows in question. She had his attention now. "Neon and metallics and lots of color." She began to pace. "We'd need new fixtures and new props. I'd need at least two of my artists back, all four would be better."

He tossed the pencil down and stood. "Keep in mind that this is the South. We move at a slower pace than New York; our life-style is gentler than Los Angeles. This is a town with lots of money and even more tradition; I don't think funky is going to work here."

Hands on hips, she squared her shoulders. "I'm not surprised you feel that way. But your view of New Orleans is much narrower—or should I say more exclusive—than mine. New Orleanians love a party and find any excuse to throw one. They down boiled seafood with as much gusto as they down beer. They host festivals and Carnival and throw cabbages on Saint Patrick's Day. As for funky, you can't get much funkier than the French Quarter at night."

Brandon held up his hands. "You've made your point. It's obvious you feel very strongly about this, but I'm unconvinced. What you're talking about is a radical change; our sales figures don't indicate that a dramatic change is necessary."

"I disagree. The Rhodes clientele is old-line New Orleans. The young, upwardly mobile consumers aren't buying from us. They're going to Saks Fifth Avenue or Macy's. Eventually our clientele is going to die off, and I mean that literally."

Her eyes were alight with the fire of enthusiasm; her cheeks were flushed with excitement. Brandon stared at her, then blinked in surprise. He hadn't recalled before how radiantly beautiful she was. Suddenly he wondered how her skin would feel against his fingertips, how her mouth would taste under his. With a small shake of his head, he dragged his thoughts back to the discussion at hand. "And you think changing our look is going to draw in the young consumers?''

She placed her hands on her hips. "Yes."

"Okay." He would see just what Veronique Delacroix was made of. "I want a full proposal, complete with department-by-department recommendations and cost breakdowns. Any questions?''

"When do you want it?" she asked, already crossing to the door.

"Next week. And, Veronique . . .''

She looked over her shoulder at him. "Yes?"

"The employee handbook has some pretty strict rules concerning tossing nudie magazines from platforms.''

"Oh?''

"Uh-huh." He sat on the edge of his desk. "Don't get caught.''

Her lips curved. Brandon Rhodes could prove to be an interesting opponent. "Got it.''

The walk from the streetcar on St. Charles Avenue to her mother's Garden District home on Annunciation took only minutes. Veronique smiled as she walked. Brandon had given her a chance. She didn't think she would be able to convince him to execute *all* her ideas, but maybe, just maybe she could convince him of a few. It wasn't a great shot, but it was better than anything she'd gotten so far.

She jogged up the steps of her mother's raised cottage. The house was modest by Garden District standards, but charming. It had been in the Delacroix family for a hundred and fifty years and had passed on to Marie when one of the aunts—Veronique never could keep all the aunts straight—died. She rang the bell.

The door was opened by her mother's housekeeper, a woman with standards that reflected her Southern Baptist upbringing. "Hello, Miss Veronique.''

"Hello, Winnie." Veronique smiled. "Mother home?''

"She's on the patio. Iced tea?"

"Please." Veronique deposited her knapsack on one of the two Queen Anne chairs that graced the foyer, then headed to the back of the house. She stepped through the French doors and onto the shady patio. As promised, her mother was there, sipping iced tea and leafing through a magazine.

Veronique didn't call out or cross the patio, but instead gazed at her. Soft-spoken and well-mannered, Marie Delacroix was the epitome of Southern womanhood. As far as Veronique knew, her mother had never raised her voice. Veronique knew for a fact that Marie had never worn slacks.

Veronique shook her head. It was hard to believe they were mother and daughter. They didn't even look alike. Veronique pictured herself, tall and thin, standing next to the tiny, curvaceous Marie Delacroix. It was almost comical.

And there was a calmness about her mother, as if she'd accepted her fate without a fight. In that way mother and daughter were most unalike—Veronique accepted nothing as fate, finding the fight one of life's most exhilarating gifts.

Veronique's smile faded. Had her father been like herself, a daredevil and a gambler, unconcerned with appearances or conventions? She'd probably never know.

"Maman," Veronique called softly, stepping forward.

Marie glanced up in surprise, her eyes warmed when she saw her daughter. "Veronique. How nice."

Veronique bent and brushed her lips against her mother's cheek; she smelled of Shalimar, and a wave of tenderness washed over Veronique. Her mother had used that scent for as long as she could remember. "You're looking well."

"Thank you. Is Winnie bringing you a tea?"

"Yes." Veronique sank onto the wrought-iron chair across from her mother.

Marie's gaze swept over her daughter. "Really, Veronique, the way you're dressed." Her tone gently reproached.

Veronique took a deep breath and counted to ten. When she trusted her voice, she said, "I came right from work. You know my job requires clothes like these."

"But still . . . ah, here's Winnie with your tea."

They were silent as the woman deposited the glass and a plate of sugar cookies. Veronique smiled a thank you; Winnie's sugar cookies were one of her favorite treats. When they were once again alone, Veronique attempted a change of topic. "How's your work for the symphony going?" She eyed the plate, then reached for a cookie.

"You've been doing that since you were a child," Marie said, her tone stern but her expression amused. "And it's quite rude."

"What?" Veronique asked, nibbling on the brown edge of the cookie. "Changing the subject?"

"Taking the biggest cookie before anyone else has a chance."

Veronique laughed. "Someone has to. Besides, it may be rude, but it's honest."

Marie hid a smile by taking a sip of tea, then dabbed her mouth with a napkin. "Now, as I was saying, about those clothes . . ."

Veronique silently groaned. Her mother, that slip of Southern gentility, could be a tenacious as a bulldog with a rib bone when she wanted something. And this was a familiar theme. "Maman, these clothes are comfortable to work in. Besides, I like them."

Marie brushed some sugar from the edge of the table, searching for just the right words. "But they're so—"

"Ugly?" Veronique inserted dryly.

Her mother's sigh was heartfelt. "You're really quite lovely, Veronique. In fact, there are times I look at you and . . ." Her voice trailed off, and she looked away.

See your father. The unspoken words hovered in the air between them. Veronique's chest tightened. She'd often wondered if her father had had the same chiseled features as herself, the same high cheekbones and arching eyebrows, the same small straight nose and widely spaced almond-shaped eyes. As she didn't resemble any of the Delacroixs, she must look like his family. But guessing and being certain were two very different things, and Veronique pushed away the hollowness that never completely left her.

After a moment she touched her mother's hand. "What are you reading?"

"Changing the subject again, Veronique?" Marie asked softly, her expression grateful.

Veronique smiled. "Yes, Maman."

Marie picked up the magazine and opened it. "I was reading the wedding announcements. The Bergeron boy was just married. It was quite a lavish party." She smiled, a faraway look in her eyes. "I'd always hoped you would..." She didn't finish the thought; her cheeks pinkened.

"What?" Veronique prompted. She glanced down at the magazine, then back to her mother in surprise. "You always hoped I'd marry someone like Robert Bergeron and have a splashy society wedding? That's it, isn't it?"

"Yes." Her mother's eyes and voice were filled with longing. "Is it so wrong to wish for you what I threw away?"

Veronique was silent. She was illegitimate in a city where lineage was everything, a city unforgiving in its prejudice. The oldest New Orleans families were like royalty; here you were judged by the high school you attended and the number of Mardi Gras courts you were invited to participate in. The social structure was clearly delineated. And she was definitely *not* one of the upper echelon.

She had no regrets. She recognized the social merry-go-round for what it was—superficial and discriminatory. She'd chosen her path years ago. What hurt was that her mother couldn't, or wouldn't, see that a man of Robert Bergeron's or Brandon Rhodes's social stature would never marry her. Not in New Orleans.

Veronique sighed. It shouldn't hurt; her mother's blind spot was nothing new. When she was a child her mother had refused to see the snubs, the barely veiled barbs, the disdain. At thirteen she'd realized that she would never change the social set's opinion of her and had stopped trying. She suspected her mother would never lose her illusions.

"No, it's not wrong," Veronique murmured, covering the older woman's hand with her own. "I know I've disappointed you, Maman. But I can only be who I am."

Marie's smile was tremulous. "You haven't disappointed me, sweetie. I just want you to have it all."

Veronique lifted her mother's hand and kissed it. "I already have it all, Maman. I promise."

Three

———

Brandon stared at the pile of thirty-year-old letters and newspaper clippings. It couldn't be true, he thought for the hundredth time since opening the safety deposit box. He gingerly picked up one of the clippings, squinting to make out faces in the yellowed and faded photograph. The caption read *Blake Rhodes and associate David Goldstein at ground breaking of new store.*

So there was some memorabilia, Brandon thought bitterly, that his father hadn't wanted framed and hanging on the wall. He set aside the photograph and picked up a letter from David Goldstein to Blake Rhodes, dated 1955. The letter proposed a partnership between Goldstein and Rhodes. A partnership in which one partner would put up the idea—a store the likes of which New Orleans had never seen—and the sweat; the other would provide the capital and the connections.

The young Blake Rhodes must have seen the potential for making a lot of money, because he answered Goldstein's letter. And the one after that. Brandon's eyes narrowed as he wondered how long, how many letters, before his father had decided to cheat Goldstein out of it all.

Brandon rubbed his temple. After going through all the papers, he'd deduced that his father had agreed to Goldstein's proposal. They set everything up using Rhodes's attorneys, and poor Goldstein hadn't been crafty enough to realize that the legal advice he was getting had been bought and paid for.

Now the only things that linked Goldstein and Rhodes were the long-forgotten newspaper article and the letters. Brandon shook his head, wondering what his father had told Goldstein when he no longer needed him. Had he been gleeful when he delivered the news that Goldstein owned none of it? Had he wielded the Rhodes name and connections, warning that the man would get nowhere in an attempt to claim what was rightfully his? There wasn't even evidence that his father had offered him money. Damn.

Dropping the letter back onto the stack of correspondence, Brandon swiveled around to face the window. Anger and betrayal welled in his chest until he thought he would burst with it. Rhodes hadn't been his father's idea at all. He'd stolen it. All the excuses he'd made to himself about his father, all the concessions he'd granted him because of his business genius had been a lie. Not only had his father not been a marketing genius, he'd been a thief.

Brandon jumped as his secretary tapped on the door then peeked in. "Yes, Maggie?"

"I just wanted to let you know that I'm leaving. Do you need anything before I go?"

"No. See you Monday."

"Good night." She paused. "Don't forget the Sovereigns' Ball tonight. Seven o'clock."

Brandon groaned. He *had* forgotten. In the light of this afternoon's discovery, a Carnival ball had been the last thing on his mind. And the last thing he wanted to do tonight. He rested his head against the high back of the chair and closed his eyes. Maybe he could make his excuses. He sighed, knowing that he would not. He was expected there; he would go.

His thoughts returned to the pile of papers in front of him. Why had his father kept all this evidence? He had to know that someday, after his death, his heir would open the box and learn the whole story. Why not destroy the lot of it and hope that Goldstein hadn't also kept the letters? Brandon thoughtfully rubbed his hand along his jaw, rough with a five o'clock shadow. When the answer came, it left a bitterness in his mouth. His father had been proud of what he'd done. His father had wanted his secret found out because he'd thought himself clever.

Brandon pressed the heels of his hands to his eyes. Maybe he'd even spent time predicting what his son would do. He could picture his old man, bushy eyebrows lowered to hide the light of anticipation in his eyes, urging Brandon to keep the whole thing a secret, to put the evidence back in the box and forget about it.

Brandon pushed away the image in his head and swung back toward his desk. He reached for the Rolodex. Poor Goldstein, he thought, flipping through the directory. Today, having a lawyer on retainer was a fact of life; lawsuits had become a national pastime. But thirty years ago people were more naive—and more trusting—about lawyers and the law. It would have been easy for a man of his father's family and money to cheat a Goldstein, especially in a town as insular as New Orleans. God only knew how many people he'd paid off.

But things had changed, and Brandon had to be sure that no one else had a legal claim on Rhodes. Fat chance, he thought, looking disparagingly at the stack of correspondence. He was almost certain that in a court of law the letters would be considered a contract and binding. His expression stern, he picked up the phone and dialed his attorney.

Two hours later Brandon stood in the doorway of the ballroom observing the festivities, his expression resigned. His being here was a testament to social conditioning and filial obedience. Tonight he was behaving the way he always had: like a proper Rhodes and the perfect member of New Orleans society.

With a sigh, he wandered inside, nodding to people as he passed. He was fed up with doing what was expected of him. He was sick to death of ritual and tradition. He slipped a finger under his choking collar and tugged. And most of all, he was damned tired of tuxedos.

Brandon took a glass of champagne from a passing waiter, motioned for him to wait, downed it and took another. It was difficult to believe, but he'd actually enjoyed the first few masquerade balls he attended. He'd thought them exciting, had thought himself important for having been invited. He knew better now; being invited had *nothing* to do with the kind of man he was and *everything* to do with his family and how much they had.

This was his fifth, and last, of the season. Thank God. Tonight was the ball of the Secret Society of the Sovereigns, an invitation-only affair, as exclusive as it was secretive.

Brandon drew his eyebrows together as the word *bunk* came to mind. He shook his head. He wasn't sure if his father's death and the discovery of his deceit was coloring his view of the world or if they had just topped off his steadily growing discontent.

His gaze circled the ballroom. Everyone looked expensive, well-heeled, chic. Plastic people. People with cultivated laughs and winter tans. People with perfect clothes and perfect teeth and perfect lives. Boring, repetitive and lifeless.

But what of himself? When had he become so civilized that dinner was inconceivable without a Rothschild or a Dom? When had he become so jaded that life had turned into a never-ending cycle of the same conversation at a dozen different parties?

He motioned to a waiter and exchanged his empty glass for a full one, then walked out onto the balcony. A storm was building; thunder rumbled in the distance, lightning flashed against the black horizon. He leaned against the railing and looked out over the French Quarter, listening to the raucous sounds of Bourbon Street.

A strange transformation had occurred in him between the ages of eighteen and thirty-five—he'd become his parents. He'd slipped into their life-style and their complacency without a fight. And he didn't have a clue how it had happened. Where had the dreams of his youth gone? Had someone stolen them as his father had stolen Goldstein's? Or had he just tossed them away without realizing their worth?

"Brandon?"

He'd recognized his mother's perfume, a special mixture from Paris, a moment before she'd spoken. Brandon turned to face her. "Mother." He inclined his head.

She laid a hand on his arm. "What are you doing out here?" She shivered and looked up at the rolling sky. "It's going to storm."

His eyes swept over her. Jeanette Rhodes, from her silver hair and crisp voice to her arrow-straight spine and severe wardrobe, was a regal woman. And a woman used to getting what she wanted. A grin curved on his lips; he held up his again-empty glass. "I'm getting drunk, Mother. Knee-walking, commode-hugging inebriated."

Her slate eyes softened; the fingers on his arm squeezed. "I understand, son. It's been difficult, I know. It was a shock to us all."

You don't know what shock is, Brandon thought, thinking of the box and its contents. He swallowed the words as he gazed down at her remarkably unlined face. His mother wasn't a particularly warm woman, but she was a courageous one. She would handle the news of his findings without so much as a pause and crisply inform him of what was to be done. He admired that quality, but he intended to handle this alone. He bent and kissed her cheek. "I'll be fine. Make excuses for me."

"As you wish," she said without hesitation, turning to leave.

"Oh, Mother..." He waited until her eyes met his. "Have a bottle sent out, would you?" She nodded, and with a rustle of silk, was gone.

Brandon stared at the empty doorway for a moment before turning back to the railing. He had a meeting with the store's attorney scheduled for tomorrow. George Sebastian was a senior partner in the oldest law firm in New Orleans and had known his father for years. No support there, he thought, curling his fingers around the railing. Although the lawyer would deny it, Brandon suspected he'd been involved from the first.

"Sir, your wine."

Brandon indicated that the waiter should leave the bottle on the wrought-iron table to his right. He handed the man a five-dollar bill. "Check on me in half an hour." The waiter nodded, took the bill and disappeared.

Brandon poured himself a glass of the sparkling liquid, turning at the sound of husky laughter. A couple had danced out onto the other end of the balcony. He watched as they twirled to the music, then as the man bent the woman over his arm in a low dip. The column of the woman's arched neck was milky against the black backdrop of night; the hair cascading down her back looked heavy and dark. Like velvet, Brandon thought, taking a sip of wine, still watching the couple. The man murmured something, and the woman laughed again, then swung away from him. As she did, she stepped into a patch of light, and Brandon recognized the patrician features of Veronique Delacroix. His eyebrows shot up. What was she doing here, and who was she with?

The man followed her and tried to pull her back into his arms. She neatly side stepped his grasp. "I said no, Peter. A dance was all I agreed to." Brandon smiled as the man's low pleading tones floated down the balcony. His smile died as the man lunged at her. Brandon started toward them, a warning on his lips. Before he'd uttered a word, the man had dropped his arms and scurried back inside.

Brandon's expression changed from one of worry to admiration. Quite a lady, he thought, picking up the bottle and sauntering toward her. "Dodging lechers is thirsty work."

Veronique spun around. "How long have you been there?"

"Long enough to see that you can take care of yourself." He handed her his glass. "What did you say to him?"

Their fingers brushed as she took the glass. Suddenly warm, she sipped the cool, tart wine. After a moment her eyes met his over the rim of the crystal flute. "I told him I'd cut him off at the knees if he dared to touch me."

"That's it?"

She lifted one shoulder. "I said it with conviction."

Brandon laughed and refilled the glass. "What are you doing here? This doesn't seem like your kind of thing."

"It's not. My mother begged me to use her invitation." Veronique turned, lifting her face to the wind. "She keeps hoping that if I attend these silly affairs, I'll either become civilized or find a proper husband." She slanted him a glance from the corner of her eyes. "What do you think?"

"I think she's wasting her time."

Her lips curved. "I think so, too." She handed the glass back so he could drink. "And what are you doing out here? All the lovelies are inside."

"Not *all* the lovelies," he murmured, eyeing her elegant profile. Damn, she was beautiful.

Her pulse fluttered. "I suppose I should thank you."

She hadn't sounded thankful at all, and laughter rumbled in his chest. Leaning against the railing, his eyes trailed over her. The wind whipped at and lifted her hair, but she didn't touch it, didn't try to smooth it. Compared to the elaborate costumes of the women inside, hers, the long skirts and tight bodice of a medieval maid, was simple and unadorned. She wore no jewelry, and her hair was simply styled, hanging free but held away from her face with a band of baby's breath. He reached out and touched one of the tiny white buds. "At first I thought you a damsel in distress," he said softly. "But now I wonder if you aren't a princess sent to brighten my night."

Veronique turned back toward him, her eyes alight with humor. She bent her knees in a quick curtsy. "I'm just a poor serving girl."

Brandon laughed. "Well then, wench, a tankard of your best ale."

She lifted her eyes coquettishly to his. "My Lord Rhodes, why would you want to drink ale when you have champagne?"

"Why, indeed?" Brandon murmured, looking down at her upturned face. Her eyes, a deep, warm brown, sparkled in the darkness. Her lips, slightly parted and tipped up at the corners, looked soft and all too inviting. He suddenly wanted to kiss her. Wanted to pull her into his arms and taste that lovely, amused mouth. He pushed the need away.

"Champagne, then." He filled the glass. "If you don't mind sharing?"

"A serving girl and a prince sharing a glass?" Her eyebrows arched. "Scandalous."

He handed her the champagne. "You like scandal, don't you?"

"Oh?" She held the delicate crystal to her lips and sipped. "What makes you think so?"

"I've heard stories." A melody, heady with saxophone, drifted from inside. "Would you care to dance?" he asked, holding out his hand.

Veronique took it and stepped into his arms, and together they moved to the music. His heart was trapped under the fingers of her right hand; its beat was sure and steady. Liking its rhythm and its warmth, she pressed closer. "What kind of stories?" He paused; she felt his shrug.

"I've heard you're . . . disrespectful."

She laughed up at him, knowing he'd abbreviated his reply, not at all stung by his words. "That doesn't sound so very bad." Lightning flashed on the horizon and the distant rumble of thunder followed. Brandon twirled her around and around. "It seems only right that I should love scandal, that I should be unconventional, even notorious. After all, I was born under the light of a reckless act of passion, a scandalous deviation from propriety."

As I was born into obligations and traditions, Brandon thought. It's only right that I'm proper and upright and . . . bored. He shook off his melancholy. "You make it sound very romantic."

"Would you rather I think of my conception as sordid? Everyone else does."

"Narrow-minded bigots don't count."

She paused, then responded thoughtfully, "No, they shouldn't." But they do, she silently added. Sometimes they count the most.

"What are you thinking?" Brandon asked, noting that her perpetually upturned mouth had thinned.

"That I love nights like this," she answered, tilting her head and looking up at the starless rolling sky. "They're energy and power. I imagine great, angry gods stopping and shouting their displeasure. The power reverberates through me, making me timid . . . and reckless."

She laughed low in her throat. "Once, when I was afraid of thunder, Maman told me the gods were bowling. She told me the rumbling was the ball going down the lane and that the loudest booms were a strike. From that night on I'd lie awake during a storm and count the strikes, keeping imaginary scores in my head and deciding on winners. I was never afraid of a storm again."

She seemed so sure of herself. Confident and somehow invulnerable. "Are you ever afraid, Veronique?" he questioned softly. "Do you ever wonder at your choices?"

"I never second-guess myself. But..." She lowered her eyes and voice. "Sometimes late at night, when the only sound in the room is my own breathing, I'm afraid." Her gaze returned to his. "Are you?"

He didn't hesitate. "Yes. There're times when I wonder what happened to the young man with dreams. When I wonder if I gave my freedom away or if someone stole it from me."

Her chest felt suddenly tight, her breath short. "And that frightens you," Veronique murmured, her voice husky with emotion. A chord, long buried, stirred inside her. It was warm and gentle, like a flower blooming after a bitter winter. "Why were you out here alone? What were you doing out here when there is a party going on a dozen feet away?"

"Getting drunk," Brandon said, breathing is her fresh, floral scent. "Thinking about life and changes and lies."

She didn't know what to say, so she said nothing. For long minutes she followed Brandon's lead, listening to the rumble of thunder and the sound of the rushing wind as they danced. "The storm's closer," she murmured finally.

"Yes." With the storm's increased fury, Brandon picked up his pace. He swung her dizzyingly toward the darkest part of the gallery, then slowed his steps until they stood the way they'd begun, bodies brushing as they swayed to the faint music.

Their eyes met and clung. Brandon swore under his breath. "This is crazy."

She trailed her fingers across his chest. "It's reckless."

"It makes no sense." Brandon cupped her face in his hands, stroking her skin in soft, slow circles.

"No sense at all," she murmured.

Her voice was low and impossibly inviting, and his gaze lowered to her mouth. "I'd very much like to kiss you. But only if you want me to."

"Yes." She lifted her face to his. "Yes, kiss me." The fingers cupping her face stilled; his head lowered.

The first drop of rain hit her cheek at the same moment her pulse began to race. The second landed on the tip of her nose just as her lips were parting. Those two drops were nature's only warning; the skies opened, releasing a flood of water. Brandon lifted his head with a jerk.

Laughter bubbled to her lips. "Do you believe in a power greater than you or me?"

Brandon sucked in a sharp, surprised breath. At first he hadn't even realized it had started raining. This crazy woman had mesmerized him. He shook his head to clear it. "What?"

Her hands still rested on his chest; his heartbeat slowed under her palm. The rain really was a shame, Veronique decided. She would have liked to kiss him. She curled her fingers into his lapels for one more moment before regretfully stepping away. "So, do you believe in God?"

She was weird, nuts, cuckoo. He reached out and tenderly touched her rain wet cheek. "We're being drenched, and you're babbling about God. Come on, let's go in."

Veronique laughed and held her ground. "Well, do you?" she pressed. "Believe in a higher power?"

"Yes. Satisfied?" He could see she wasn't and groaned. In a gesture of resignation, he lifted his eyes heavenward. What did it matter? He couldn't get any wetter. At least the downpour had slowed to a steady rain.

"I need more champagne," she announced. "How about you?"

"Why not?" He leaned against the whitewashed siding; his eyes crinkled at the corners as he watched her. Her sodden gown dragged the ground as she sashayed down the balcony. She grabbed the bottle, dumped the rainwater from the glass and refilled it with wine. She sipped, then made a face. "Flat, warm and watery."

"Mr. Rhodes?"

Brandon glanced at the doorway. It was the waiter, carrying a fresh bottle of champagne. His expression was horrified.

"You said to check on you..." The man's voice trailed off. "Shall I leave this?"

Brandon made a small fluttering motion with his right hand. "No. Thank you for—"

"Yes," Veronique inserted firmly, and stepped forward. "We'll take it." She took the new bottle from the tray and set the old one in its place.

"Yes, of course. Well, I..." The waiter cleared his throat, his eyes racing between the two of them. He obviously thought them both insane. "Perhaps I could get you some towels?"

"No."

"Yes." The waiter coughed, and Brandon repeated the affirmative. "Yes. Some towels, please."

"I like being wet," Veronique said after the man had left. She wrestled with the cork. "I used to sneak out when it started to rain—Maman would think I was playing quietly in my room—and I'd roll in the wet grass, sail boats in mud puddles and generally make a mess of myself. It was great."

"Here, let me." Brandon took the bottle from her hands and popped the cork. It sailed into the air, and the wine bubbled over the lip of the bottle. He poured a glass and handed it to her. "First of all, I can't imagine you playing quietly in your room. Secondly, didn't your mother ever catch on?''

"She's a sweet, trusting soul." Veronique's nose twitched as she took a sip of the effervescent liquid. "Besides, the housekeeper had a soft spot for dirty little hoydens. She'd hustle me upstairs and clean me up before Maman, or worse, Grandfather Jerome, caught sight of me."

Brandon thought of the forbidding Jerome Delacroix and winced. His father and Jerome had had business dealings, but he'd never trusted the man or understood why his father did. And he couldn't imagine Veronique living in the same house with him. "How long did you live with Jerome?"

"Until I was thirteen." She handed him the half-full glass. "Then Maman inherited her house. No one could convince me that where you live doesn't make a difference. Our lives changed drastically for the better. What's your story?"

Brandon shrugged. "Military school. Harvard Business. I was a page in the Mardi Gras court of Rex when I was twelve..." His voice trailed off as he thought of his father and the contents of the safety deposit box. Suddenly frustrated, he ran both hands through his dripping hair. "I don't have any bad-boy stories to tell. I've never been crazy. Or disrespectful. Or irresponsible. Dammit, I *feel* like being irresponsible." He looked up at the clearing sky, then over at Veronique. "I feel like taking chances."

Empathy, warmth...genuine liking poured out of her for him. Veronique's eyes met his. "You've come to the right place. I specialize in irresponsible; chance taking is my forte." She arched one delicate eyebrow. "Would you like me to show you?"

Brandon's eyes met hers a moment before he laughed. "Let's have some fun."

Her lips curved into a wicked smile. "Are you prepared to accept the consequences?"

"Which are?"

"Well," she began, "it depends on the agenda, but you can count on a killer headache tomorrow, an empty wallet tonight and lots and lots of regrets."

His smile answered hers. "Where do we start?"

"Right here." Veronique took the glass from his hands, downed the champagne, then set it aside. "First rule, wild people rarely drink champagne, but when they do, it's right from the bottle."

"No problem there," Brandon said, and held the bottle to his lips. Because of the fizz, it was like drinking Coke from the bottle, but with a lot more kick. "Now what?"

"Now we exit this dead party and go have some fun." She rubbed her hands together. "I know this place that—"

"Excuse me, Mr. Rhodes, madam, your towels."

Veronique eyed the man speculatively as she took one of the towels. "Is there a way out of here besides the ballroom?"

The waiter blinked, as if surprised by the question. "Only through the kitchen, but—"

"Perfect," she interrupted, her tone crisp and business-like. "Can you show us?" When the man nodded, she grabbed Brandon's hand. "Come on. Don't forget the wine."

The waiter led them back into the ballroom from the darkest side of the balcony. Veronique glanced around and grinned. Even skirting along the edges of the room, they were drawing attention.

"I'm disillusioned," Brandon whispered as the waiter ducked through a door tucked in a deserted corner. "I thought wild people would parade right through the middle of the ballroom."

"No way," she whispered back, sticking close to their guide. "Then they'd all know what we were doing. Sneaking out is so much more effective: the few who saw us will spread the word, and everyone will wonder what we were up to. Conjecture and hearsay are far more dangerous than the truth.''

As she finished speaking, they stepped into the kitchen. It was a beehive of activity. Waiters rushed in and out, depositing empty trays, then picking up freshly-filled ones. The cooks mixed, checked and arranged. The caterers hovered and fussed, barking out an occasional order or curse.

They didn't draw as much attention as she would have expected, considering what they must look like. Both caterers shot them nasty glances; she heard one of the dishwashers mutter, ''crazy rich folks.''

Their waiter-guide stopped at a gray metal door with an exit sign above it and held out his hand. Brandon dug in his pocket and pulled out a bill. ''It's wet,'' he murmured apologetically.

''It'll dry.'' The young man smiled as he slipped the bill into his pocket, then turned and walked away.

''Ready?'' Brandon asked, hand on the doorknob.

''Yes...no...wait.'' Veronique breathed deeply and sighed. ''I just noticed something. It smells incredible in here.'' Her stomach rumbled. ''I haven't eaten. How about you?''

''No, but—''

''I suspect we can scrounge something up.'' She was wandering toward the counters covered with trays before she'd even finished speaking.

Minutes later Veronique sighed and licked her fingers. ''A feast,'' she said as she finished one hor d'oeuvre and eyed the platter heaped with mushrooms stuffed with crabmeat, crawfish pastries, delicately seasoned shrimp and a countless variety of canapés. ''I'm in heaven.''

Brandon watched her lick one finger after another. Desire hit him with the force of a hurricane hitting land. He wanted to take her hand and clean the juices from those fingers himself. Saying the first thing that came to mind, he tried to push away the erotic images flooding his head.

"Speaking of heaven, why did you ask me if I believed in God?"

The canapé stopped halfway to her lips. Her laughing eyes met his. "Because, for whatever reason, we weren't meant to kiss. Fate, destiny, the gods were working against our lips meeting."

His eyes rested on her mouth, damp from her own tongue. His abdomen tightened. "That's the silliest thing I've ever heard."

"Not at all." She popped the hors d'oeuvre into her mouth and immediately picked out another. "It wasn't meant to be. I'm a great believer in—"

Without warning, he tumbled her into his arms. Her startled brown eyes met his determined gray. "Believe in this," he murmured a moment before his lips settled over hers.

The hors d'oeuvre slipped from her fingers; her hands instinctively flew to his chest. He brushed his lips softly against hers, as if testing their texture and their taste. Veronique moaned low in her throat as he continued to nibble at her mouth as if it were one of the canapés she'd just devoured. Frustrated at the teasing touch, she curled her fingers into his lapels and pressed closer.

But Brandon wouldn't be rushed. He took her mouth leisurely; it was a slow, thorough seduction. Without words he coaxed and wooed. With the lightest of caresses, the most soothing of movements, he conquered her. His hands and lips had never left her face, yet it seemed as if no part of her had been left untouched. Veronique wondered if she would ever feel steady again.

Brandon had felt her surprise, her instinctive resistance. He'd liked catching her—the spontaneous, mercurial Veronique—off guard. But more, he liked the way she melted against him. The blood rushed to his head as her lips softened, then parted. She tasted of champagne, laughter and the subtle blend of spices in the canapé she'd just eaten. The taste was addictive, and he dove deeper. She smelled of rain and flowers; he breathed in the heady combination and knew he'd never experienced a more alluring scent.

Veronique slid her hands up to cup his neck. She was used to flash fires and lightning. She understood passion, expected explosion. But this tender command, this steady, hot flame was new to her. He drew her in as the waves drew in the sand, rhythmically, inevitably. The kiss lasted only moments, Veronique felt as if she would be changed forever.

She sucked in a quick, surprised breath as he pulled away. She didn't like, nor was she accustomed to, being caught off guard. She would have to be careful around Brandon Rhodes; he could prove to be dangerous.

Veronique stepped away. Her tone was light as she said, "You're learning. Kissing in the middle of a kitchen filled with curious eyes—scandalous! This incident will be all over town by morning."

Brandon didn't comment. His spontaneous act had startled him more than her. Kissing her had been like witnessing an explosion. He suspected making love to her would be like being the dynamite. He wasn't sure he was ready for dynamite.

Veronique shifted from one foot to the other. This situation was awkward, and she liked awkward even less than startled. What was he thinking? She tossed her head. She absolutely would *not* act like a ninny over a simple kiss. She groaned silently—there'd been nothing simple about that kiss.

"So...?" Brandon stretched the word into a question.

"So," Veronique said, trying to sound glib, "we better get going. It'll be dawn before we know it." She grabbed his hand and started pulling him. "I know someone who's having a Bacchus bash tonight. The god of wine and revelry—it seems appropriate, don't you think? Come on, if we hurry, we might catch the last of it."

Four

Brandon stirred restlessly, then groaned. He was warm, he ached, he felt cramped. In an attempt to get comfortable, he rolled onto his side. Something wasn't right—the bed felt too soft, the pillow too hard, the blankets too short.

But there was an inviting softness against his cheek, his shoulder, the back of his thighs. And that scent. His lips curved as he breathed deeply through his nose. It was a fragrant, lingering scent—subtly earthy, endlessly sweet. Like a woman.

His eyelids flew up. As the light hit his bloodshot eyes, a shaft of pain shot through his head. Groaning out loud, he squeezed his eyelids shut. My God, how much had he drank? he wondered. He felt as if he'd been hit by a wrecking ball. The hammer inside his head tripled its beat, and he groaned again.

Brandon cautiously turned his head. The movement caused another sharp pain, but this time at the base of his skull. Gritting his teeth, he slowly opened his eyes, ready for but still cursing the sting of light. It took a moment, but when his eyes focused, they focused on the creamy flesh and soft curves of Veronique Delacroix.

Brandon blinked. It couldn't be, but... He shook his head, then blinked again. It wasn't a mirage—Veronique was next to him in bed, warm, naked, utterly relaxed. Desire hit him with the subtlety of a tidal wave hitting shore.

Heart thudding in his chest, he fell back against the mattress. Damnation. He might have just had the most exciting night of his life, and he couldn't remember it. Sometimes life just wasn't fair.

Brandon lay there a moment, then unable to help himself, sneaked a peek at her. From his position all he could see was the curve of her shoulder, her lovely profile, the suggestion of a body under the blankets. Feeling like a voyeur, Brandon propped himself on an elbow so he could gaze down at her sleeping face. There were the lightest of smudges under her eyes, giving her a sultry, shadowed look. Her unpainted lips were the color of an almost ripe strawberry; her hair fanned across the pillow like a tangled web of silk. Curious, he reached down to capture several strands; her hair felt the way it looked—soft and silky.

Brandon cocked his head. She was impish even in sleep, he thought. Her mobile mouth tilted at the corners, and she looked as if she could laugh at any moment. He liked that. His eyes lingered. That mouth was entirely too kissable. He wanted to take it while she still slept, wanted her to awaken with her lips still warm from his and his taste on her tongue.

As he leaned down to do so, she made a sound that was a cross between a whimper and a moan, then flopped onto her side. The blanket fell away from her shoulder revealing not the soft white flesh he'd expected, but soft white cotton. He let out a long, disappointed breath. Veronique was wearing a T-shirt. It was one of those skimpy white ones with spaghetti straps. Sexy, but compared to what he'd thought the blanket was hiding...

Brandon frowned thoughtfully. Maybe he couldn't remember making love because they hadn't. He sucked in a deep breath, then peeked under the covers. "Underwear," he muttered, sighing. He lay back against the pillow and threw an arm over his eyes. Nothing had happened. They hadn't made love; he hadn't missed the most exciting night of his life. It was for the best, really. He hadn't planned to...it'd been the furthest thing from...He lifted his arm and slanted her a glance from the corner of his eyes. He sighed again. If she hadn't planned to seduce him, why had she brought him here?

He sounded petulant even to himself, and he grinned. It was for the best. She was kooky and irresponsible; she had no place in his traditional world. Besides, he suspected Veronique Delacroix could prove to be addicting. One taste could lead to an all consuming need.

He couldn't afford such a distracting habit. One night of chance taking and walking on the wild side was enough to last a lifetime. And it *had* been wild, he realized, bits and snatches coming back to him. The bacchanal had been their first stop. The party had taken place at a decaying mansion on Esplanade Avenue. Pedestals with life-size papier-mâché replicas of all the Roman gods had been set up around the pool.

Bacchus himself had been portrayed by a short, balding man with a huge potbelly. He'd worn a wreath of grape leaves on his head and almost nothing else. A dozen people had been costumed as satyrs. Togas, feathers and wine had been supplied in abundance. Brandon winced as he remembered sticking his head into the red-wine fountain; his tux would never be the same.

At least he'd drawn the line at wearing a toga. He frowned. Good thing. If he'd been wearing a sheet, that Greek sailor he'd challenged to a game of pool, the one who'd been a very poor loser, might have beaten him to a pulp instead of only threatening to do so.

Their next stop had been The Dungeon. Open only from midnight until dawn, it had been populated with characters straight out of a Franz Kafka novel. After that, there'd been Bourbon Street and dancing in the street; they all ran together in a confusing mix of images, scents and flavors.

Brandon listened to Veronique's deep, rhythmic breathing. His expression softened. At the heart of it all had been Veronique—her energy, her enthusiasm, her humor. Yes, indeed, she could become a most distracting habit. Take today for example... Today! Brandon's eyes few to his watch. It was already 11:40. He had a meeting with Sebastian in two hours and twenty minutes. He had better get going.

So as not to awaken Veronique, he cautiously pushed the blanket away and began to slip out of bed. Just as his torso cleared the sheets, Veronique moaned and rolled over. He cursed under his breath and settled back onto the bed. Her cheek rested against his shoulder, her arm lay across his chest and one of her impossibly long legs was cradled against his. He could either wake her or wait it out. Yawning, Brandon decided a few more minutes wouldn't hurt.

Veronique smiled into Brandon's shoulder. In the past ten minutes he'd tossed and turned, groaned, sighed, moaned and muttered. She suspected he was uncomfortable and eager to leave. That's why she'd rolled over.

Well, he'd gotten what she promised. She knew for a fact that his wallet was empty—she'd had to pay their cab fare home—he'd drunk enough that if he didn't have a killer headache he wasn't human, and judging by the noises he was making he had lots of regrets.

Veronique bit back a laugh. She couldn't blame him. Last night had been almost too weird, even for her. The hosts of the bacchanal had been friends of friends, and she hadn't known just what to expect. Brandon had blanched when he saw where the party was being held; he'd almost called it quits when he caught sight of Bacchus himself, flitting around in nothing but a loincloth fashioned to look like a fig leaf.

But then he'd surprised her. She didn't know if he'd had too much to drink or if he'd just decided to let go, but he'd become a wild man. She still couldn't believe he'd stuck his head in the wine fountain or picked a fight with a two-hundred-pound Greek or paid a street musician to play "The Yellow Rose of Texas" so they could dance. At four in the morning she'd poured him into a cab and brought him home with her.

Her lips curved. Undressing him had been a delight. He had a beautiful body; even now she longed to pull the covers away so she could gaze at him—not touch him, just a long, leisurely gawk. Last night, for one insane moment, she'd considered taking advantage of him. But she'd been a good girl and had crawled under the covers and gone to sleep. Boring.

She took a deep breath. He smelled like a man should—not flowery and artificial like men's colognes, but like sweat and musk and that indefinable something that every woman recognized and responded to. She breathed in again; her blood stirred even as she acknowledged it was time to let her captive go.

Veronique propped herself on an elbow and gazed down at him. Her lips twitched. Despicable, she thought. She deserved every nasty rumor that had been spread about her; she deserved to be flogged. His eyes opened slowly; they were red-rimmed and wary as they met hers. "Good morning, darling," she murmured huskily.

Darling? "Morning," he muttered.

Veronique walked her fingers up his chest. "How do you feel?"

Brandon frowned. Was there a hidden meaning to that question? She'd practically purred it. He decided to play it safe. "How am I supposed to feel?"

"Why—" her voice lowered even further "—wonderful, of course." An unexpected thrill ran down her spine as his eyes darkened.

Brandon swallowed past the lump in his throat. Maybe something *had* happened. Maybe they'd put clothing back on after... no, nobody did that. But still—

Veronique trailed a finger along his jaw. "Poor Brandon, you look positively haggard."

But she didn't. His gaze swept over her. In fact, she looked as fresh as a spring morning. Another bad sign. "Why don't you?"

"Why don't I what?" she murmured suggestively, barely swallowing a laugh.

Brandon squirmed. She was too sexy for her own good. "Look haggard," he said, sounding grouchy.

"Because, my darling, I didn't overindulge. If you'll remember, after we left the Sovereigns' Ball, I stuck to either juice or Perrier for refreshment. Besides—" her smile was the most intimate and wicked she could muster "—I have every reason to look wonderful."

Brandon scowled. His head was killing him, and he was tired of being the mouse to her cat. And the plain truth was he didn't want to know if they'd made love. Because if they had, he would want to again. And he didn't think that was a good idea. "I have to go. I have an appointment."

Veronique sat up, feigning petulance. "We haven't had a chance to talk." She plucked at the blanket. "And we haven't had breakfast."

Breakfast—another sure sign. His determination waivered, and he cleared his throat. "I'd love to have breakfast another time. But I'm meeting with George Sebastian, the store's attorney, in an hour..." He tossed back the covers and got out of bed.

Veronique fell back against the pillows. Her shoulders shook with contained laughter as she watched him fumble with his clothes. She had him on the run. Her expression changed from amused to admiring. He really did look good in his shorts. She folded her arms behind her head. A woman could get sidetracked from the game at hand by those legs.

"But I'll call," he continued, trying to sound reassuring but coming across as nervous. "We'll go out. Really, I...where's my shirt?"

"Don't know." Her eyes crinkled at the corners. "My guess is somewhere between Esplanade Avenue and Bourbon Street."

Brandon's head jerked up. "Excuse me?"

"You took it off after it was soaked with red wine," she explained patiently. "Don't you remember?"

"No." He dragged a hand through his hair. "Then what did I wear?"

She lifted a shoulder. "Your tie and jacket, your slacks and...that."

He looked down a the colorful object laying on the chair. It was a plastic headband with long loose springs attached. On top of the springs were glitter-covered balls. He picked it up. Now he remembered—no shirt on his back and dealie bobs on his head. A regular freak show.

"You looked sexy, take it from me." She rolled onto her side. "I use one of my grandfather's old shirts for a painting smock. If you don't mind the odor of turpentine...it's in the kitchen closet."

"Thanks." He put on his socks, then stuck a leg into his pants. "Did anyone I know see—damn." One of his trouser legs was inside out, and he cursed again under his breath, dropped his pants and started over.

Veronique caught her bottom lip, breathing deeply through her nose to steady herself. He would be furious if she laughed. When she trusted herself to speak, she said, "You know, I think photographers are the first thing we should decide on. A good photographer can make or break—"

Brandon's head snapped up. He'd just maneuvered the first leg into the now right-side-out trousers. "What?"

"Photographers," she said slowly, as if explaining something to a child. "Of course, our trip to Uptown Finery shouldn't wait too long. And a jeweler—"

Brandon stared at her as if she'd lost her mind. "What the hell are you talking about?"

Veronique stood and walked toward the bathroom. When she reached the door, she looked back at him. "Why, darling, I'm talking about our wedding plans." His jaw dropped. She laughed and blew him a kiss. "I think I'll take a shower."

Veronique shut the door behind her, then leaned against it, overcome with laughter. She'd played dirty, taking advantage of his hangover and nonexistent memory of the night before. The poor guy didn't know what had hit him.

Wiping her eyes, she crossed to the shower and turned on the water. She was just giving him what he'd wanted: a night of irresponsibility and a morning of regrets. Okay, maybe she'd taken it too far, but anyone who put their night in her hands had better expect her best shot. Humming under her breath, she turned on the shower, then slipped out of her T-shirt and panties. Besides, she'd call him later and—

Her head snapped up as the bathroom door flew open. She gasped and grabbed a towel. Brandon stood there, her painting smock half-buttoned, his expression thunderous. "Brandon! I'm not dressed."

"What do you mean, 'wedding plans'?"

Veronique held back a grin. She was a terrible tease; she just couldn't help it. "Which word didn't you understand?"

One look at the devilry in her eyes and he knew the truth. There had been no proposal; indeed, nothing at all had happened last night. She'd been having a little fun at his expense. Well, what was good for the goose.... He took two steps into the room. In a honeyed voice, he murmured, "I thought we might clarify our relationship."

Veronique held the bath sheet in front of her with both hands. Her chin tilted. "I hardly think now is the time to discuss—"

"Who said anything about a discussion?" He unbuttoned one of the shirt's buttons and took another step closer.

He was bluffing. She was sure of it. Her brows arched. "Then what are you saying, darling?"

He didn't answer. Instead he finished unbuttoning the paint-splattered shirt and shrugged out of it. His eyes met hers. "What I'm saying...darling...is I don't want to talk at all."

Veronique's smile faltered. He couldn't be serious. Surely he didn't mean... This time when he took another step, she backed up.

"In fact, I'd like a reminder of last night." He took another step. "I'm a little fuzzy about the details."

The ceramic tile was cold against her naked back. She cleared her throat. "I could fill you in another time. The shower is...you see..."

Brandon's eyes lowered to her hands. "No, unfortunately I don't see. Perhaps if you got rid of the towel?"

My God, he was serious. "No," she said firmly, tightening her grip on the lavender terry cloth.

"Considering what you intimated we shared—" he reached out and hooked two fingers around the top of the towel "—don't you think it's a little late for modesty?" He tugged, and she inched forward. It was either move or lose the towel. "In fact, after last night, isn't it a little silly that I'm not taking a shower with you?"

Veronique held fast to the towel. "Yes...no..." His fingers brushed against her breast; her flesh turned to fire under his touch. "You'll be late for your appointment," she improvised in a last-ditch effort to get him out of her bathroom. As she uttered the words, she felt like a fraud; the last thing she wanted him to do was leave.

"To hell with the appointment." His eyes lingered on her breasts.

Veronique squirmed as she realized her nipples were hard. She wondered if he could tell. "I think..." Her voice shook, and she cleared her throat. "I think..."

"What, Veronique?" He pulled her closer. "Do you think we should make love again?" His voice deepened; their eyes locked. "Here?" The length of her was pressed against him now. He could feel the hard points of her breasts through the terry cloth, could feel the way her body trembled. And he saw the arousal in her darkened eyes, on her heated cheeks.

Veronique searched for something to say. She couldn't think, couldn't seem to focus on anything but Brandon. Her senses swam with his words and his warmth.

"Well, Veronique?" His lips grazed her eyebrows, her cheeks.

"Well what?" Her level stare was ludicrous in light of the husky timbre of her voice.

"We could make love in the shower—" he paused; his voice deepened "—on the floor."

The blood rushed to her head until she was dizzy with it. His words raced along her nerve endings; they tingled with expectation. He'd mesmerized her. She told herself to pull away, she told herself to resist; the message never reached her brain. Her head was filled only with wanting Brandon, his touch, his taste, the pleasure she knew he would give her. Towel forgotten, she reached up and threaded her fingers through his hair.

He lowered his head, but stopped a fraction of an inch from her lips. "You shouldn't start games you aren't pre-pared to finish," he whispered, laughter in his voice. He caught her sultry bottom lip between his teeth as he wrapped the towel around her, tucking it in at the side of her breast, then pulled away.

Her eyes fluttered open; they were glazed with passion. He resisted the urge to catch that inviting mouth again. "Better take your shower before the hot water runs out." He picked up the shirt and crossed to the door. His smile was wicked as he said, "Thanks for last night, even though nothing happened." He softly shut the door behind him.

Veronique's legs were suddenly weak, and she sat on the edge of the tub. She took a deep, steadying breath. That rat. That double-crossing, dirty-playing son of a ... Her lips curved. He was good; she had to hand it to him. He'd startled her, then knocked her so firmly off balance she'd never even seen him move in for the kill. She shook her head. She'd underestimated him.

Veronique checked the water, then made a sound of disgust. It was cool; he *had* had the final word after all. She twisted off the faucets, stood and walked back to the bedroom. Flopping down onto the bed, she stared at the ceiling. She still couldn't believe she'd fallen for his ploy. Like a novice or an ingenue. It'd been a long time since anyone had gotten the best of her. A corner of her lips lifted. Oh, she'd deserved it. Every manipulative word and gesture, plus some.

The amusement faded from her lips and eyes. She would have to do something about this ridiculous attraction she felt for Brandon Rhodes. They were all wrong for each other; they had nothing in common. She rolled onto her side. The bedding still smelled of him. She breathed deeply, and her pulse quickened. She'd have to wash all the bedclothes today, she thought, trailing her finger over the crisp percale, feeling surrounded by him.

This attraction was just a silly trick her hormones were playing on her, Veronique decided, her lips tilting. That, or the work of some malevolent spirit. It would pass, and her life would be back to normal. Sure. She was almost over it already.

Her smile vanished as she wondered what Brandon was doing at that very moment.

"Sebastian." Brandon held out his hand in greeting. "Thanks for meeting me on such short notice."

"No problem," the older man said, gesturing toward his cluttered desk. "I work every Saturday morning; this hasn't inconvenienced me in the least. Have a seat."

Brandon would have preferred to stand, but he sat anyway. Despite his raging headache, his queasy stomach and foul mood, he had a surplus of energy. He felt antsy and on edge, and he wasn't sure why.

"You look like hell. Something wrong?"

Brandon's eyes snapped back to the attorney. He was a small, slim man with thinning silver hair and a neatly trimmed mustache. Brandon didn't dislike the man, but he'd never really liked him, either. "Hangover," he said shortly.

The attorney nodded sympathetically. "I've had a few of those myself." He folded his hands in front of him, becoming all business. "When you called you mentioned a safety deposit box and some documents?"

"Yes." Brandon opened his briefcase and took out an envelope. He opened it and handed the bundle of papers inside to Sebastian, then sat back and watched. The older man slipped on his glasses and slowly began flipping through the papers. He paused every now and then for a second glance, drawing his eyebrows together momentarily.

After several minutes he took off his glasses, tapped them on the stack, then looked up at Brandon. He cleared his throat. "I don't know where to begin."

"So, you *did* know about this?" Brandon's expression was tight.

"Yes. And no." He leaned back in his chair. "I wasn't your father's attorney at the time this occurred. He came to me five years later, when Rhodes was a huge success and he was thinking of opening another store. Your father was getting cold feet," the man said simply. "Retailing is a high-profile business, and the business was obviously making a lot of money. He was thinking of expanding and was scared to death that David Goldstein was going to pop up any second and take it all away."

A muscle jumped in Brandon's jaw. "What did you advise him to do?"

"To wait," Sebastian said quietly.

For a moment Brandon sat in stunned silence. "Wait for what, for God's sake? After hearing and seeing the evidence you told him to do nothing? I don't believe this."

Sebastian tossed down the pencil he'd been toying with. "What could he do? Five years had passed. The man had never again approached your father, indeed he wasn't even in town. To track him down and offer him money would have been an admission to guilt." He held up his hands to stop Brandon's reply. "Yes, your father was guilty. But he could have been prosecuted. He could have lost it all. And for what? The deed couldn't be undone."

Let sleeping dogs lie, Brandon thought. He stood and walked to the window; Sebastian's wife was cutting flowers. He looked away. "What happened then?"

"We hired a private detective to find David Goldstein and keep tabs on him. It turned out he'd died the year before in an automobile accident." The attorney idly picked up the newspaper clipping, then as if uncomfortable with the image, set it back down. "He might have eventually approached your father and demanded what was rightfully his... We'll never know."

"So, my father was off the hook," Brandon murmured. It was too clean. And that made him nervous. "What about a wife... children?"

Sebastian coughed and looked away. "He never married."

Brandon's eyes narrowed. The man was being evasive. "What about children, Sebastian?"

The silence crackled between them. After a moment the older man sighed. "David Goldstein was Jewish, smart and from the wrong side of the tracks. He became involved with a girl from a prominent Catholic family. The disparity in their families' social and financial positions was bad enough, but thirty years ago a marriage between a girl of the Catholic faith and a boy who was Jewish was...well...was out of the question."

There was a tightness in Brandon's chest. He had a feeling he wasn't going to like what came next. He flexed his fingers as Sebastian started talking again.

"The girl's family found out about the affair and were furious. To make matters worse, she'd become pregnant. Her father was blind with rage and shame. He totally blamed Goldstein and was determined that his daughter would never see him again." The attorney's voice was suddenly tired. "In his mind no husband was better than a Jewish husband. He elicited your father's help in running Goldstein out of town."

"It all worked out rather neatly, didn't it." Brandon's voice was brittle. He'd thought his father many things, but a liar and a cheat had never been among them. "My father was a hell of a guy, wasn't he? He cheated his partner out of his half of their business, his girlfriend and unborn child, then ran him out of town. Great."

Sebastian's expression softened. "I understand how you feel, and believe me, I would rather not have had to tell you. If it makes you feel any better, to this day I'm not sure whether your father had planned to cheat Goldstein out of his part of Rhodes before the girl's father approached him or whether—"

"Don't bother. It won't make me feel better. It's done now." Brandon took a last look out the window then crossed to the desk. His voice was low as he asked, "How did they do it? How did they run him out of town?"

Brandon saw the distaste on the other man's face. "They framed him for a crime he didn't commit. The sheriff was a family friend with daughters of his own and—"

"And he was in on it," Brandon finished. "Paid off?" When Sebastian nodded, Brandon picked up the newspaper clipping and stared down at the yellow, faded image. So tragic. The poor bastard had lost everything. He met the other man's eyes once again. "Who was the girl, Sebastian?"

The lawyer stood up. "Let it rest, Brandon. These events happened thirty years ago. Don't stir up past hurts, past dirt. The way it stands now, Rhodes is secure. No one can take it away from you because no one, not your mother or the girl or her father, knows the whole truth. Just you and I. Let it die here."

Brandon's lips tightened. That was the problem—he didn't know if he could live with the knowledge. "Who was she?"

The determination in Brandon's expression convinced the older man to give up. He sighed. "Marie Delacroix."

Brandon blanched. "Marie Delacroix?" he repeated stupidly. It couldn't be.... It wasn't possible.... That would mean that Veronique was David Goldstein's only offspring.

"Yes."

Brandon sat down. He remembered the expression in Veronique's eyes when she'd said, "I didn't know my father, either." He thought of her voice as she'd asked, "Would you rather I think of my conception as sordid? Everyone else does." He laced his fingers together thoughtfully. He knew who Veronique's father was. He could tell her...

But to tell her about her father, he would have to tell her about his own father and what he'd done. What would she do with the information? Brandon sighed and stood. He had a lot to think about. "I appreciate your time and honesty, Sebastian."

The attorney stood and walked him to the door. When they reached it, he laid a hand on Brandon's shoulder. "I know you don't want to hear this, but I'm going to say it anyway. Your father built Rhodes from nothing—"

"Nothing but an idea," Brandon interrupted, his voice cold. "An idea he stole."

"That's right. But he built Rhodes into what it is today. He put in all the money, years of hard work and sweat. If Goldstein had remained his partner, who knows if the store would have done as well. Maybe they would have sold out or gone their separate ways. Who knows? Believe this, Brandon, your father deeply regretted the actions of his youth. He would have given anything in later life to have made amends with Goldstein. Consider those things before you take action."

Brandon's eyes met the other man's. Both their expressions were solemn. "Don't bother to show me out, Sebastian, I know the way."

Five

After ten days Brandon still wasn't sure what to do. For his own peace of mind he knew he had to try to make amends for his father's actions. He stared out his office window and frowned down at Canal Street. He would tell Veronique the whole story and offer her a substantial sum of money for the wrong that had been done to her father. It wouldn't undo the action, but perhaps it would equalize it a little bit. At least he would be able to sleep.

Brandon regretfully turned away from the window. He'd had difficulty concentrating since the Sovereigns' Ball; it seemed all he'd done was stare out the window and think about his father and Veronique and a thirty-year-old drama. He sat down behind his desk and pulled out the Dallas file. The preliminary marketing report was in, and the research was favorable. By all indications a Rhodes in Dallas...

How would Veronique react to his offer? He rubbed his throbbing temples. He could more imagine her making a public stink, going to the papers and filing suit than keep-

ing quiet. He may be furious and disillusioned over his father's deceit, but he didn't want his father's memory or the
Rhodes name destroyed by a scandal.

Brandon's expression softened. He liked Veronique. She
made him laugh and forget responsibility. She was warm
and unpredictable and giving. But a colorful past and a nose
for fun weren't qualities one looked for in a business partner. Nor did they instill confidence in him that she would
react logically to his offer or make a businesslike decision.

Brandon gave up the pretense of working and closed the
Dallas file. Leaning back in his chair, his thoughts returned
to Veronique. Today she was presenting her proposal for the
display department; she would arrive any minute. He'd only
seen her once in the last ten days, at a department heads'
meeting. She'd been wearing pencil-leg jeans, high-top
aerobic shoes, a sleeveless sweatshirt and a straw cowboy
hat. When she'd looked up at him and smiled, he'd wanted
her so badly he hurt.

Brandon shook his head. This fascination with Veronique was crazy. He knew it was linked to his father's death
and his own grief and that it no doubt had to do with his
need for a change of pace and his boredom. But rationali-
zation didn't lessen the ache of wanting or expel her from his
mind.

Maggie buzzed him; the Miami store manager was on line
one. *What now?* He picked up the phone and greeted the
man, all the time wondering if Veronique had thought of
him at all in the last ten days.

Veronique peeked at the nameplate on the receptionist's
desk. "Hi, Maggie. I have an eleven-thirty appointment
with Mr. Rhodes."

The receptionist looked at her over the top of horn-
rimmed glasses; Veronique smiled and the woman's expression warmed. "He's on the phone right now. Take a seat,
and I'll tell him you're here as soon as he's off."

"Thanks." Veronique sank onto the small, striped sofa and crossed her legs. After a moment, she realized she was clutching her proposal and set it carefully on the coffee table. She would never admit this to anyone, but she was nervous. She, the daredevil and gambler, was anxious about showing Brandon a bunch of numbers on a page. Her palms were even sweating. It was silly.

It didn't feel silly, though, and she looked down at the envelope and resisted the urge to pick it up and go over the material one last time. This was her chance to really put her mark on the store. Her chance to make something that was a reflection of herself, something that would last.

Veronique sighed and recrossed her legs. If she were being honest, she would admit that she was on edge about seeing Brandon again. She couldn't forget their last encounter, had replayed every word, had examined every response. And she wasn't a woman who analyzed. The blasted man had bested her! He'd made her feel submissive and yielding and totally, achingly alive.

She glanced down at her hands. He hadn't called. She'd expected him to, and he hadn't. She'd done nothing over the last ten days but think of him, and he hadn't even bothered to call. She was annoyed—with him and herself.

Maggie stood. "Mr. Rhodes will see you now."

Veronique smoothed her short, straight denim skirt, then picked up her proposal and followed. The woman opened the door to Brandon's office and stepped aside so Veronique could pass. Brandon was sitting behind his desk; he stood and held out his hand when she entered. She wished the sun wasn't behind him so she could read his expression.

"Veronique. How are you?" His gaze raced over her with a greediness that shocked him.

She lightly clasped his hand; her pulse fluttered in response. She silently swore. She was getting tired of feeling like a teenager who'd just discovered hormones. "Fine. And you?"

"Just fine."

"Survived your hangover?" Veronique could have bitten her tongue when she saw his smile. He was no doubt remembering their last encounter.

Brandon's lips tilted as a picture of Veronique wearing nothing but a towel shot into his head. He'd been a fool to walk out of that bathroom. "I had a few bad hours, but, yes, I survived."

They stood there, hands clasped and eyes locked, for long moments. Veronique was the first to break the contact. She cleared her throat. "Well..."

Brandon looked down at their joined hands. How long had they been standing there? He was behaving like a lovesick schoolboy, and it wasn't a role he particularly liked. He dropped her hand. "Shall we begin?" he asked, his voice cool and businesslike. He motioned her to take the seat opposite his, then sat down. "So, what do you have for me?"

Veronique inhaled deeply to clear her head, then began. "This proposal represents what I feel are the optimum changes for the display department. My suggestions can be modified up or down. Rather than explaining it to you in detail, I'll let you see for yourself." She handed him the proposal, then held her breath as he opened it and began reading.

Modify up? Brandon wondered in shock as he skimmed over the figures. He didn't think this proposal could be made any more elaborate or expensive than what she'd already outlined. His eyebrows rose in surprise, then lowered ominously. My God, what would she do if she *did* own half the store and could make these kinds of decisions herself?

Brandon's gaze lifted from the page in front of him to meet hers. "This is ridiculous—twenty thousand dollars for one mannequin?"

Ridiculous? Veronique's spine stiffened. She should have expected that type of response from him. He was a stuffy, uptight businessman with no creative vision. "It's the latest technology,'' she explained, her tone controlled. ''An automated mannequin. It's programed for a series of motions—''

''A robot?'' Brandon's tone was incredulous. ''You want to buy a robot?''

''Actually, I'd like to buy several, but thought we could try one first. Ours would be the first in New Orleans. Think of the sensation it would cause in the front window.''

''I can't get past the sensation it would cause down in accounting.'' He shook his head. ''Veronique, two neon fixtures at five thousand each?''

''For juniors and young men's,'' she said evenly. ''An upbeat look is essential in those two departments.''

''Fourteen new mannequins? Architectural columns and facades?'' She was the most unbusinesslike woman he'd ever met. This made as much sense as hiring criminals to man the cash registers. ''Faux boulders? Adobe pots and figures? Mylar? This is way too costly. It adds up to—''

''One hundred and ten thousand dollars.'' Talk about robots. The man was a close-minded, corporate automaton. She wanted to slap him. Veronique clasped her hands in her lap and warned herself to keep cool. ''But that figure represents the cost of buying all those items outright. There's always the—''

''You can rehire two of your artists,'' Brandon interrupted, closing the proposal. ''Order four new—*un*automated—mannequins.''

''That's it?'' Veronique asked aghast. She hadn't been there ten minutes, and he was already rejecting her ideas.

''I'm sorry, Veronique, but—''

She stood and faced him angrily. ''You never had any intention of considering my ideas. Did you just want to see me jump through hoops?''

''That's as much nonsense as this proposal. You may be the artist, but I'm the businessman. And I'm telling you this makes no financial sense.''

Idealistic artist, logical businessman. The blood rushed to her cheeks. "If you'd bothered to hear me out, you'd see that purchasing the items I listed was only one of our options. There's a business called The Display Warehouse in L.A. They specialize in new upbeat props and fixtures. Everything I named in the proposal is available from them by the month. And they're quite reasonable. For example, the automated mannequin would cost us two thousand a month. We could rent it for peak shopping times like Christmas and back-to-school."

"I'm sorry, Veronique."

"This would make perfect sense if you'd consider the long-term increase in..." She paused when she saw his face. His expression was as closed as his tone had been. He was dismissing her. Veronique placed her palms on the desk and leaned across it. "You're as arrogant and opinionated as your father was."

A muscle jumped in his jaw. "And your head is in the clouds." They glared at each other across the desk. Her cheeks were wild with color, her eyes narrowed with determination. Brandon's eyes unwittingly lowered to her mouth. Good God, he realized in shock, he wanted to kiss her. Even now, frustrated at her unrealistic ideas and furious over the comment about his father, he wanted to taste that lovely, angry mouth. Instead, he yanked his gaze away. "Why aren't I surprised at your totally unrealistic view of this situation?"

With a loud huff, Veronique straightened. She couldn't believe she'd ever been attracted to him. "There's no talking to you. Your closed mind is made up." She stuffed her proposal back into the envelope and headed toward the door.

Brandon came around the desk after her. Grabbing her elbow, he swung her back around. "I could fire you."

She lifted her chin defiantly as the blood pounded in her head. "Go ahead."

"Don't tempt me." That was the problem. His lips curved despite his anger. Everything about her tempted him. He was better off letting her walk out the door; she wasn't for him. "Leave the proposal, Veronique. I'll give it another look."

"Another look or real consideration?" She saw the answer in his eyes and tucked the envelope more firmly under her arm. "Don't bother."

She stepped through the door, then snapped it shut behind her. The reception area was empty; Maggie must have gone to lunch. Veronique wrinkled her nose and glanced down at the desk. There was a still-smoldering cigar butt in the ashtray. Nasty things, Veronique thought. There was no accounting for some people's taste. Tilting her chin, she strode from the room.

Three days later Veronique was still seething over Brandon's rejection of her proposal. She hadn't seen him, but he'd been on her mind a lot. She'd been considering various forms of petty and childish revenge, and at the moment Chinese water torture seemed like a rather nice choice.

She grinned as she pushed open the glass door to Jack's Eatery, a greasy spoon located in the heart of the central business district. Of course, she hadn't totally eliminated the rack or thumbscrews. She was a woman who liked to keep her options open.

The bell above the door jingled as she stepped into the empty restaurant. Sunday morning in the CBD was not a peak dining hour for Jack's. Poor Jack, Veronique thought, the only business he did on weekends were regulars like herself and the occasional businessman who had to catch up on work and got hungry. But she suspected Jack didn't mind too much; he only opened because he had nothing else to do.

"Hey, Jack," Veronique called out, "you've got a customer." She settled onto one of the stools at the counter and looked around. She loved this place. It was vintage fifties, complete with a black-and-white tile floor, individual juke boxes at each booth, shiny chrome and pink vinyl. A big, burly man in his mid-fifties came out of the kitchen. His smile was as broad as his waistline. "Hey there, little gal. I wondered if you'd be in this morning."

"Jack," Veronique's tone teasingly reproached, "would I miss a Sunday?"

"Oh, I don't know—" he swiped at an imaginary water mark on the counter, then looked back up at her, his blue eyes alight with humor "—I keep thinking one of these days you'll find a fella who has his own ideas about Sunday mornings."

Veronique feigned horror. "No way, Jack. This is a tradition, a way of life, a ritual. No one will ever come between me and Sunday mornings with you." Her smile widened. "Got any blueberry waffles back there?"

Jack laughed and shook his head, then poured her a cup of coffee. "One of these days, little gal. One of these days..."

Veronique smiled to herself as she added cream and sugar to her coffee. Maybe Myra Elson from upstairs would be interested in meeting Jack. With his penchant for coddling and hers for independence, they would be an interesting couple. Tucking the idea away for future consideration, she pulled her newspaper from her knapsack.

She hadn't been teasing about Sunday mornings at Jack's being a ritual. She always came in between nine and ten, always ordered waffles, bacon and a half a grapefruit and always sat at the counter and read the paper. Even the way she read the paper was a tradition. First the society gossip column, then the comics, then the sports section. After that it was up for grabs. She grinned as she added yet another packet of sugar to her coffee. The gossip column was her favorite. It was like a soap opera in print, and she loved tuning in to see who was doing what to whom.

Veronique took a sip of the hot, sweet liquid, then pulled out the society section. *Mrs. Sidney Barlow donated a lesser known Monet to the New Orleans Museum of Art.* Veronique could smell the bacon Jack was frying in the kitchen and her mouth began to water.

Sarah and Candace Dupree are dating titled twins they met while vacationing in the Riviera. Titled twins? Tacky. Veronique took another sip of coffee. *Rumor has it that Lily St. Germaine is getting a five-point-six carat diamond solitaire for her thirty-fifth wedding anniversary.* I wonder who started that rumor, Veronique thought dryly. She skimmed the next two listings. Where was the good stuff? Ah-hah, here we go. *A little bird told me that our very own Bachelor of the Year, Brandon Rhodes, spent a wild—dare I say even bawdy—night with none other than the notorious Veronique Delacroix. Moreover, my informant hinted that the couple never said good-night.* Veronique's mouth dropped in surprise. *Could there be more than fun and games going on between this unlikely couple? Or is our handsome bachelor merely proving his prowess?*

"Here you go, little gal." Jack set the overloaded plate in front of her. "Hey, is something wrong? You look like you've seen a ghost."

Veronique's eyes met his. "No, Jack, I'm fine. Just hungry."

"Well, dig in. I'll be in the kitchen if you need anything."

"Thanks." As soon as he was out of sight, she pushed her plate away. Her eyes returned to the paper, and she reread the blurb. There was only one "little bird" who could have given Sissy this information. Brandon. No one else knew about their night together. Her eyes narrowed. That rat. That no good son of a . . .

One corner of her mouth lifted. She had to give it to him, it was one hell of a move. He'd outmaneuvered her again, and very neatly at that. He'd gotten back at her for the prank she'd played on him, plus he became notorious by association. And he didn't even have to spend more time with her.

She couldn't let him get away with it. She drummed her fingers on the counter. What could she ... publicly call his bluff. She almost laughed out loud when the thought came to her. The perfect comeback. Brandon would backpedal as fast as possible. She could picture his expression—surprised, disbelieving, shocked. Oh, yes, turning the tables on Mr. Brandon Rhodes would be interesting. Now all she needed was a plan.

Suddenly starved, she dug into the cooling waffles.

Fifteen minutes away, Brandon sat in the courtyard of Commanders Palace Restaurant, reading the Sunday paper and having brunch. He'd started with an appetizer of shrimp sautéed in butter and garlic, followed by Eggs Sardou. The French bread, with its crunchy crust and light-as-air center, was not only authentic, but was still warm from the oven. The coffee was as black as night and as thick as cream; it was served in a small silver pot that was left at the table.

Brandon didn't look up as the waiter deposited his chocolate mousse, then refilled his coffee cup. His eyebrows drew together. He didn't like what the Dow Jones had been doing lately. Erratic at best, he thought with a small shake of his head. At this rate ...

"Brandon, what a lovely surprise."

He lifted his eyes and silently groaned—Lily St. Germaine. She could stir up more trouble than any three people he knew. And she was obviously excited about something. She had the look of a bloodhound on the trail of tenderloin, and he had the uneasy feeling that he was it. "Hello, Lily."

"How's your mother? Holding up, I hope." The woman's gaze sharpened. "And how are *you*?"

The question was ripe with anticipation. Brandon ignored it. "Fine," he answered shortly. "We're both fine."

"You must be very busy. We rarely see you these days. In fact, I didn't even run into you at the Sovereigns' Ball . . . or did I?"

This time Brandon's gaze sharpened. "What are you getting at, Lily?"

"Nothing, nothing at all." She gestured gaily with one hand. "Just catching up. Claude and I have always been fond of you."

Right. And cats love water. Brandon arched one, dark eyebrow to acknowledge the lie. "Look, Lily, if there's—"

"So, are you seeing anyone special?" she gushed. "Anyone *different*?"

Brandon's eyes narrowed. The stress she'd placed on "different" couldn't go unnoticed. Lily was a notorious gossip, and this was leading to something. "No, Lily, no one special. Why do you ask?"

The woman clucked her tongue. "Now, Brandon, you know I don't like repeating gossip. Claude's waiting, I must go. Enjoy your mousse."

Brandon watched her leave, his expression thoughtful. Gossip? About him? She couldn't be referring to the Bachelor of The Year thing—that was old news. *News* . . . of course. The Sunday society section was the biggest, and juiciest, of the week. He pulled out the Vivant section of the paper, then opened it to the gossip column. It took him a moment to find it; he read it twice, then burst out laughing. *Where in the world had Sissy gotten this story?*

Veronique. It had to be. He shook his head, not at all annoyed over the blurb. Veronique was miffed over his criticism of her proposal, so she'd decided to play another trick on him. He was surprised she hadn't told Sissy they were engaged. Now *that* would have caused a stir.

He folded the paper and sat back in the chair. It was a shame there wasn't something going on between them. Besides the obvious reasons, it would give him a chance to get to know her better. Maybe then he could accurately gauge her reaction to the information about her father and his connection to Rhodes.

He could ask her out. Dinner, dancing, the whole bit. Brandon shook his head. She would refuse. He didn't have to ask to know that. The only thing that little hellion never turned down was a challenge.

That was it. His lips curved into a smile. He would turn the tables on Ms. Veronique Delacroix, call her bluff and start courting her. It would serve her right and give him the time he needed. He drained his coffee cup, then replaced it on its saucer. This could be fun.

Pleased with the turn of events, he motioned for the waiter to bring his check.

Six

_____

It was Friday before Veronique had a chance to initiate her plan. Brandon had been out of town all week—he'd flown to Miami on Monday, then to Atlanta on Wednesday. His secretary had turned out to be an extremely chatty woman and, therefore, a wealth of information. She'd even said what time Brandon would be getting in Friday morning.

Veronique had considered meeting him at the airport in a limousine with champagne on ice, but had decided that that wouldn't be a public enough gesture. Besides, it would have been too early in the morning for champagne, and without it the prank's effect was greatly reduced.

So, today was the day. Veronique made one final check in the mirror before she headed up the escalator. She'd dressed with care, choosing one of her most outrageous outfits: black bodysuit, black sneakers, and a long, loose-fitting overshirt made of clingy T-shirt material patterned with leopard spots. She'd knotted the shirt at the bottom on the right, thus revealing a generous length of spandex-clad thigh. She smiled. If this outfit didn't knock him off balance, nothing would.

The ride up the escalator took only moments; she saw Brandon the moment she reached the top. He was talking to the buyer of better dresses and the store manager. Veronique took a deep breath. She suddenly felt as if she'd run up the flight of stairs. Just nerves, she told herself. Nerves and anticipation of the game.

She walked determinedly toward Brandon. It looked as if his discussion was breaking up, and she increased her pace. It wouldn't do if there were no witnesses. "Hello, everybody," she said as she reached the trio.

"Hi, Veronique." The buyer, Margo Vincent, looked appraisingly at Veronique's outfit, then as if Veronique had passed muster, she smiled. "I like what you've done with window number two. Very imaginative."

"Thanks, Margo." Veronique sidled up to Brandon and slipped an arm through his. It was a possessive gesture, a gesture that spoke of past intimacy. She felt Brandon's arm stiffen under hers, and from the corner of her eye, saw the surprised glance that followed. She swallowed a laugh. "So, how was your buying trip? Anything extraordinary?"

The other woman jerked her gaze from Veronique's hand on Brandon's arm to her eyes. She flushed, and Veronique could almost hear the speculations dancing through her head. "Why, yes. I was just telling Brandon and Tom about the unusual..." While the woman talked, Veronique sneaked repeated and adoring glances up at Brandon. One time, when his eyes met hers, she mouthed the words "I missed you." As she did, Margo stumbled over her sentence. But even better was the stunned look on Brandon's face. Perfect.

Veronique turned her attention back to Margo. "Sounds like it was a profitable trip. I especially look forward to seeing the new Kamalis. They sound like window one material." Veronique slipped her hand out of the crook of

Brandon's arm. As she did, she lovingly stroked the sleeve of his jacket. "Chip's waiting for me up front..." Her words trailed off, and she met Brandon's eyes once again. "Don't forget," she whispered, her voice husky, "Mimi at Uptown Finery is expecting us at three-thirty." Uptown Finery was New Orleans's most exclusive—and famous— bridal and couture shop.

Tom cleared his throat; Margo stifled a gasp; Veronique turned to walk away.

Before she could, Brandon caught her elbow, swung her around and pulled her against his chest. He glanced over at the wide-eyed couple. "Excuse us for a moment, will you?" His lips curved into a slow, wicked smile as he gazed down at her. It was her turn to look stunned, he thought with satisfaction. She'd given him the perfect opening, and he was going to use it. "How could I forget?" he asked, his voice low and caressing. His fingers drew slow, sensual circles against the small of her back.

Awareness raced up her spine at the same moment her mouth dropped open in surprise. She ignored the first and remedied the last. It took only seconds to regain her composure; when she did her eyes narrowed. "Darling, if you'll—"

"When will you learn," he continued, still stroking her back, "that I never forget anything...not about you...or about us."

Veronique's mouth was suddenly dry; her heart hammered against her chest. She frantically searched for something to say, willed herself to look away. He didn't give her the chance. He tipped his head and his mouth captured hers. She flattened her hands against his chest and emitted a small squeak of surprise. What was he—she couldn't believe he— in the middle of the store?

With the speed of a flash fire, surprise was replaced by need. Her mouth softened, then parted. He tasted faintly of mouthwash; Veronique found the minty flavor addictive and dove deeper. The scents of his morning shower clung to him; Veronique wondered if she would ever again be able to bathe and not think of him. She curled her fingers possessively into the lapels of his jacket.

Brandon smiled against her lips, lingering for a moment over the sweetness of her response, then regretfully drew away. "I warned you once about starting games you weren't prepared to finish," he whispered so only she could hear. Then louder, "I missed you, too."

Veronique took a deep, steadying breath, then glared at him. She wanted to hit him—he'd done it again. He was insufferable. She smiled sweetly. "I'm glad."

Her smile couldn't hide the temper in her eyes, and Brandon laughed softly. He slipped his hands down her back and gave her fanny a quick familiar pat. He heard her intake of breath, felt the fury ripple through her. "Run along, darling. I'll see you at three."

Veronique bit back an angry retort. He was treating her like a brainless twit. Like a groupie or a...a bimbo. Well, she wouldn't let him get away with it. Retaliation now was impossible, but she could wait. And the winning would be sweeter for it. Her smile was saccharine. "All right, darling," she said, before blowing him a kiss and walking off.

Late that afternoon Veronique stood at the sink in the display department washing paint brushes. Mardi Gras's gaudy colors—purple, green and gold—ran down the drain. She was still steaming over the outcome of this morning's skirmish. How did he continually manage to surprise her? Veronique shook her head as she worked the soap through the brush's bristles. She wouldn't let him catch her off guard again.

The corners of her mouth lifted in wry amusement. She'd made her move with subtlety and innuendo—she'd tried for a little class. She could have brought up mud wrestling or pool-hall brawls, but she hadn't. Brandon, on the other hand, had been direct and as subtle as a Sherman tank. Really, kissing her in the middle of the store?

Her cheeks warmed, and she scowled as they did. Dammit, she'd liked it. The whole thing—possessively slipping her arm through his, his lips on hers, the husky timbre of his voice. And she didn't want to—couldn't afford to. If she grew to like it she could be . . . hurt.

Veronique went to work on the last brush, viciously working the soap into a lather. That wouldn't happen. She could remain objective, impartial. All she was dealing with were a few raging hormones. She'd handled them before, and this time would be no different. She was in control.

Veronique rinsed the brush and set it next to the others on the rack to dry. The metal double doors scraped open behind her, and she called out, "Chip, why don't we stop for a beer at the River Bottom on the way home."

"Isn't it going to be tough to be in two places at once, Veronique?"

At the sound of Brandon's voice, Veronique spun around. She acknowledged the shaft of irritation that he'd surprised her again. With deliberate impudence, her gaze roamed over him. He'd exchanged the suit he'd been wearing earlier for a pair of black jeans and a long-sleeve pullover. The pullover was also black, made of nubby cotton and open at the throat. He looked casual, comfortable and sexy as hell, she admitted with a frown. It was going to be difficult to remain objective if she kept noticing the way the soft fabric clung to and outlined his thighs. She raised her eyebrows. "What are you doing down here? Slumming?"

His eyes met and held hers as he crossed the room. "That was nasty, Veronique. You're usually better than that." He stopped in front of her, smiling. She looked annoyed. He was getting to her. "Great stunt this morning. Unexpected and effective."

"Thank you." She turned and dried her hands, taking a moment longer than necessary to do so. She tossed the paper towel into the trash and turned back around. Her eyes were cool as they met his again. "You've surprised me, Brandon. Twice now. And I don't like surprises."

"Oh?" He shoved his hands into his pockets. "What do you plan to do about it?"

The amusement in his voice made her blood boil. She didn't even blink. "Make sure it doesn't happen again."

He laughed and gave in to the urge to reach out and touch her flushed cheek. The flesh was soft and hot under his fingers. "I called you cocky once; you haven't done anything to change my mind."

She stepped away from his hand. His touch was much too distracting. "Really, Brandon, compliments are so embarrassing." Turning, she picked up her purse, a huge shiny vinyl tote stamped to look like crocodile hide, and slung it over her shoulder. "You never did say what you were doing down here."

"I would have thought it was obvious." He took her arm. "Ready?"

Veronique slanted him an amused glance from the corners of her eyes; she couldn't help herself. "May I ask for what?"

"We don't want to keep Mimi waiting, do we?"

Veronique laughed and shook her head, certain he was bluffing but willing to play along. They walked toward the door. "You know, by now the fact that you're down here is all over the store. And this morning's encounter, well I wouldn't doubt that Sissy's drooling over it right now." He opened the door, and she stepped through it. Laughter bubbled to her lips. "I can see it now—the scandal continues...illegitimate, notorious Veronique Delacroix corrupts Mr. New Orleans, Brandon Rhodes. I'll be tarred and feathered."

"You say that as if you'd enjoy it. This way." Brandon touched her elbow to steer her toward the elevator that led to the parking garage. What was he up to? She followed his lead and stepped into the elevator. He punched five, then folded his arms across his chest and looked at her.

Veronique resisted the urge to stare up at the floor numbers as they were illuminated; instead, she held his gaze. "So, are you ready to tell me where we're going?"

"I already did."

Veronique's eyes crinkled at the corners. "Mimi at Uptown Finery, right?" Brandon just smiled, and Veronique laughed. "Whatever you say."

The doors slid open; they stepped out of the climate-controlled elevator and into the muggy garage. It reeked of exhaust and mildew. She followed Brandon's lead, stopping with him next to a shiny black Porsche. The top was off, the windows down. The interior was a natural-colored leather and smelled like it. "Magnificent," she murmured, running her hand lightly along the front quarter panel.

"You want to drive?" Brandon grinned and held out the keys. Without a moment's hesitation, she plucked them from his fingers and slid behind the wheel. "Ever drive one of these before?" he asked, watching as she checked the wipers and turn signals, as she adjusted the seat and mirrors. She was all business.

"Not this model. Buckle up." She pushed in the clutch and turned the key. The car roared to life. She took a moment to test the shift pattern, then shifted into reverse and backed out of the parking space. Moments later they were heading down the winding concrete tunnel.

Brandon tightened his fingers on the armrest as she took the final curve doing thirty. "Why do I have the feeling this is the biggest mistake of my life?"

Veronique laughed. "It's too late to start worrying now. Besides, I promise you'll live to regret it. Mimi?" When he nodded, she crossed Canal Street and headed uptown. They were silent as she maneuvered through the late-afternoon traffic. She slipped in and out of lanes, ran the yellow lights whenever possible and shouted at pedestrians who crossed against the light. When they'd cleared the worst of it, she tossed him a quick teasing glance. "See? Safe and sound."

"The trip's not over yet," Brandon returned dryly.

Veronique just laughed. Although she could have taken St. Charles or Carondelet, she chose Tchoupitoulas Street. It was a winding, sometimes rutted road that ran along the Mississippi River. It was lined with warehouses, some decrepit, some renovated into restaurants and clubs for the World's Fair, others into condos. Farther uptown on Tchoupitoulas renovations gave way to rows of dilapidated shotgun houses and businesses that depended on the river for support. More than one resident lolled on his front porch or steps, enjoying the afternoon sun and watching traffic; a group of teenage boys stood in front of a corner restaurant, drinking Coke and clowning around. It was an old street, a street, Veronique thought, with character. Even though it was out of the way, she traveled it whenever possible.

She flashed Brandon a smile as she took a curve with a speed designed to leave him breathless. "I cut my teeth on high-performance cars and have never lost my taste for them. It's like gambling, it gets in the blood." The wind whipped her hair around her head. She pushed it away from her face and laughed. "I borrowed Grandfather's Jag once. I'd just gotten my license; Jerome had stopped by to see mother. The keys were in the ignition. I couldn't resist."

Brandon turned toward her. His gaze softened. She looked completely content, utterly relaxed. He'd been teasing when he'd said he worried about her driving. She handled the car skillfully and with absolute control. And her fondness for speed hadn't surprised him. She was a woman who embraced experience, who enjoyed living on the edge. It seemed right that she should be behind the wheel of a fast car, laughing and breaking the law with the wind flying through her hair. Brandon smiled to himself; he was getting sentimental. "What happened?"

"Grandfather reported the car stolen. They picked me up just as I was cruising Pontchartrain Beach." She swerved to avoid a pothole. "He was furious, but when I explained that he should be grateful that I took the car instead of a real thief and that he should be more careful in the future, he went wild." Her laughter mixed with the sounds of the street, the hum of the engine and the rush of the wind. It was a sound filled with life. "He didn't press charges, but only because Maman begged. Although, he did try to convince her to send me away to a girls' school. From that time on, when he came to visit he made sure his keys were in his pocket."

"I'll bet he did," Brandon murmured, chuckling. "Jerome Delacroix isn't the most magnanimous man I've ever met."

"Especially about his possessions," Veronique inserted. "You should have heard him the time he found me playing in the Rolls—"

"That's it!" Brandon snapped his fingers. "I thought all this sounded familiar; years ago I heard a story about you and Jerome's Rolls—"

"Fabricated," Veronique said with a wave of her hand. "The gossip mill changed the Jag to a Rolls, added boys, liquor and a crumpled fender to the story." She turned onto Magazine Street, then almost immediately onto St. Charles Avenue. "It was the first time I had an exclusive in Sissy's column."

"From humble beginnings . . ."

Veronique's eyes met his, and they laughed in unison. The next few minutes passed in silence. From the corners of her eyes, Veronique watched Brandon. He fiddled with the radio, then leaned back in his seat, eyes closed, totally relaxed. He was an unusual man, she decided. A man not what he seemed, a man of contradictions. She shook her head slightly. She'd thought he would be society stiff and big-business tough, but he was warm and funny and likable. It was too bad she was just along for the ride, she thought with more than a twinge of regret.

Veronique pushed the unwanted sentiment away as she turned into Uptown Finery's parking lot. Located on St. Charles Avenue in an old Victorian mansion, the shop boasted a client list as old-line and blue-blooded as Uptown itself. In fact, this store had become such a New Orleans tradition with the wealthy that Rhodes had been forced to discontinue its bridal department.

Veronique parked the car and turned toward Brandon. She didn't conceal the humor lurking in her eyes. The ball was in his court. "What do you propose we do now?"

He knew what she was doing, and he wasn't about to fold. "Go in," he answered simply.

Veronique lifted her brows in surprise. "You know, it's going to look pretty silly if we go in there and don't buy something. Uptown Finery is not an 'I've just come to browse' sort of place."

"So we'll buy something."

Veronique shook her head. Follow the leader had not been one of her favorite childhood games, but if he insisted on digging his own grave, what could she do? Laughter bubbled to her lips. "I'm not going to make it easy for you."

"I'd be disappointed if you did."

"All right. It's your money and your reputation. Just let me brush my hair," she said, not bothering to look in the mirror but knowing it was wild from the wind.

Brandon leaned over and tangled his fingers in the silky mass. He rubbed the strands between his fingers; his eyes searched her face as he did. With her wild hair and flushed cheeks, she looked as if they'd just made love. His lips curved into a satisfied smile. "Leave it," he murmured, dropping his hand.

For a moment she'd thought he was going to kiss her. Her fingers flexed on the wheel as she swallowed her disappointment. Dammit, she'd wanted him to. She still did. She wasn't comfortable with the want and was unsettled by the disappointment. He opened the car door for her, and she stepped out. Taking a deep breath, she smiled convincingly and took his hand. Together they crossed the shell lot toward the building.

There was a wreath made of dried wildflowers and ribbon on the flawlessly finished cypress door. Brandon rang the bell. The door was opened by a woman in a crisp white apron and cap. "Good afternoon." Brandon handed the woman his card. "Mimi is expecting us."

The woman nodded and ushered them into the front parlor. While she got them settled and asked if they would like some refreshment, Veronique looked around. The room was large, with glistening wood floors and fourteen foot ceilings. It was furnished with pieces from the same era as the house, carrying through the atmosphere of faded grandeur.

Veronique had been in this room only once before. Her mother had been determined she have a sweet sixteen party and a gown to go with it. Veronique had been determined there would be neither. The afternoon had ended with her mother angry and embarrassed and Veronique in tears. Her expression clouded. She'd won the battle—there'd been no party. But she'd never forgiven herself for humiliating her mother in front of her peers, and she'd never again crossed the line between independence and willfulness.

"What's wrong?" Brandon asked softly. She suddenly looked so sad. He reached out and cupped her cheek. Her skin was as soft as a Georgia peach, as flawless as silk.

Veronique unconsciously tipped her head into the caress. "I made a scene here once...." Her voice trailed off, and she willed away the unhappy memory. There was nothing to be gained by reliving the past. "I was just thinking how bratty sixteen-year-old girls can be," she finished, her lips curving into a wistful smile.

Brandon was glad to see the shadows disappear from her eyes. He dropped his hand. "When I was sixteen I thought they were pretty great."

"I'll bet you did," Veronique murmured as Mimi swept into the room. She was a tall, striking woman, with the dramatic coloring and aristocratic features of her Creole ancestors.

"Mr. Rhodes, I'm Mimi Latour." The woman held out an elegant hand. "Welcome to Uptown Finery."

"It's a pleasure." Brandon grasped her hand. "My mother has spoken very highly of you."

"Of course." The woman turned toward Veronique; her eyes swept over her. "How may I be of service?"

Veronique decided that she'd been right as a child—follow the leader wasn't much fun. She looked up at Brandon, batted her eyelashes coquettishly and said, "We need a gown for our engagement party."

Brandon put his arm around Veronique and pulled her into his side. "Now, darling, you know it's actually an engagement announcement party."

"Yes." Veronique placed her palm lovingly on his chest. "We're engaged to be engaged. I want the whole world to know."

"But it's a secret," Brandon added quickly, looking at the older woman. "No one knows, not even our families."

Veronique had to hand it to him, he was quick on his feet. Three generations of Latour women had built this business on as many clandestine affairs as legitimate ones. Mimi, like her mother and grandmother before her, could be—and would be—as discreet as the grave. Veronique stood on tiptoe and kissed his cheek, whispering as she did, "You're a crafty one, aren't you?" Brandon's answering smile said more than words could.

"Ah..." The woman's eyes moved speculatively from Brandon to Veronique and back. When she spoke, her warm words belied what Veronique was sure she was thinking.

"How wonderful to be in love. Your secret is safe with us. Girls!" The woman clapped her hands, and two teenage girls appeared at the door. Mimi turned back to Veronique and Brandon. "Gretchen and Susan will show you up to the Rose Room. I'll join you directly."

As they followed the two tittering girls, Brandon leaned down and whispered in Veronique's ear, "By the way, feel free to make a scene."

Veronique swallowed a laugh and shot him a pouting look. "I'm devastated—I've already started and you haven't even noticed."

"Ten bucks says you can't find the ugliest dress in this place in—" he checked his watch "—under an hour."

Veronique eyed him suspiciously. "Who decides if it's ugly enough?"

"We both have to agree."

"Make it twenty and you're on."

Thirty minutes later Veronique groaned. It didn't look good for the home team, she thought, eyeing the newest rack of dresses. Everything so far had been either understated and elegant or nauseatingly pretty. She'd finally instructed Mimi to bring in everything she had. The room was bursting with dresses.

"Ugly is in the eye of the beholder," Veronique muttered as Mimi held up a pink tafetta with ruffles.

"Now, now, darling, we both have to agree." Brandon's tone was deliberately mild. "And I think that's a lovely dress. Mimi, set that aside, will you?"

Veronique scowled at him. "I'd look like a piece of birthday cake in it." She stood, crossed to the rack of dresses and flipped through them. "Really, Mimi, these just aren't me. I had something a little more...unusual in mind. Something louder...something... Wait a minute, what's this?" Veronique pulled out the gaudiest dress she'd ever seen. Apricot-colored and decorated with an overabundance of spangles and rhinestones, it was floor-length and sleeveless, with a plunging neckline. She smiled. "It's perfect. What do you think, Brandon?" Veronique held it in front of herself and whirled around.

"It's pretty ugly," he admitted, grinning.

"The ugliest." She turned back toward the frowning woman. "We'll take it."

"Oh, no..." Mimi said, obviously distressed. "That dress is for another type of occasion...an awards banquet or even a Mardi Gras ball, but not for an engagement...it's too eccentric..." Her words trailed off at Veronique's determined expression. "If you'll step into the dressing room so we can fit it," she said, disapproval dripping from each word. "Susan and Gretchen will help you."

In less than a half an hour the dress had been fitted and paid for. Gloves and shoes dyed to match had been ordered. Veronique had tried on a dozen hats, but none of them had been tasteless enough to go with the dress. Laughing, they'd left the boutique and, at Brandon's suggestion, had headed across the street for a drink.

They sat at one of the sidewalk café's wrought-iron tables. The red-and-white patio umbrellas were a festive spot against the backdrop of pavement and brick. Even though it was five o'clock, the sun was still bright and hot. But the edge had been taken off, Veronique thought, lifting her face to its gentle heat.

Traffic noises mixed with the music spilling out of the café and the conversations from the surrounding tables. City sounds. Familiar and exhilarating. She was as at home in a place like this as most people were in their kitchens. Veronique leaned back in her seat and smiled. "Taking money from you is getting to be a habit. If you're not careful, you'll end up broke." Just then the waitress arrived with their drinks: Bloody Marys, hot with tabasco and fresh-ground pepper. After the young woman had deposited the drinks and a basket of pretzels, Veronique handed her the twenty she'd just won from Brandon, then shot him an amused glance. "I still can't believe Mimi showed eyelet, lace and tafetta to a woman wearing a black bodysuit." She popped one of the tiny pretzels into her mouth and crunched it between her teeth. "Does that make any sense?"

"I still wish you'd tried on the pink." Brandon laughed and stirred his drink with the celery stick. "I would have liked to have seen you as a piece of birthday cake."

"It wouldn't have been a pretty sight; ruffles make me very nervous." Her laughing eyes lifted to his. "And mean."

"Poor Mimi." Brandon paused to sip the fiery drink. "The whole time, I knew she was thinking of how shocked my mother was going to be by our news. I'm surprised she didn't ask *us* to keep quiet about our visit to her."

The shaft of irritation was as quick as it was unexpected. He was right. Mimi had remembered her—her business hadn't become such a success by forgetting customers—and she'd been pitying Brandon's mother her future, oh-so-unsuitable daughter-in-law. And she *would* keep quiet about their visit because Brandon had asked her to... and because she knew it wouldn't be good business to be associated with such an improper liaison. "Yes," Veronique repeated, an edge to her voice, "poor Mimi. I'm sure she's shaking in her Jourdan pumps right now."

Brandon shot Veronique a sharp look. She'd sounded so cynical just then, and cynical wasn't her style. What was she thinking? He reached across the table and took her hand. Turning it over, he stared at the tiny network of lines on her palm for long moments. He wished they would tell him what he needed to know.

"Are you trying to read my palm?" she asked with deliberate lightness.

"In a way," he murmured, running his thumb along the delicately ridged surface. "I'm curious about you," he said as he stroked the smooth, translucent flesh of her wrist. Her pulse scrambled under his finger.

Veronique held his gaze. "Oh?" The sound, breathless and feminine, belied her even glance. Annoyed with herself, she cleared her throat.

"Mmm-hmm." He slid his fingers from her wrist to toy with hers. Her hands were long, slim and strong; the nails were smooth and gently rounded. There was a tiny cut on the tip of her index finger; he lifted her hand to his lips and placed a kiss there. "I've wondered," he murmured, lowering her hand, "what it was like for you growing up without a father." He felt her fingers stiffen under his and softly stroked them.

At his words, her eyes lowered to their joined hands, then moved uncomfortably away. She could reply glibly; it wouldn't be the first or the last time she did so in connection with a question about her father. She'd mastered the snappy comeback years ago. But she didn't want to do that, Veronique admitted to herself. She wasn't sure why, but she wanted to share a part of herself with him.

When she spoke, her voice was low and sad. "I used to fantasize about him," she began. "I imagined him as tall, strong and handsome. He would sweep Maman and me into his arms, telling us it was all a mistake, that he *did* love and want us." A smile touched her lips. "Often in my fantasy, he would challenge Grandfather Jerome to a duel to avenge our honor."

Veronique picked out a pretzel and stared at it for a moment before dropping it back in the basket. "When I got old enough to understand the birds and bees, my fantasies changed. I'd look at my friend's fathers and wonder 'is he the one?' I'd pick out the best-looking men everywhere we went and spin tales about them being my father. And always there was some mistake, some soap-opera twist of fate that had kept him from us." Her eyes lifted to his. "Silly."

"No," Brandon murmured, not quite sure what to say. Her fantasy was closer to the truth than she would ever guess. He felt like a total jerk for keeping the truth from her.

But he didn't have a choice. The future of Rhodes was on the line. Uncomfortable, he shifted in his seat.

"Yes, silly," Veronique repeated. "And childish. When I realized that I'd never be able to change old traditions and even older prejudices, I gave up fantasizing about my father and began living for myself. I know now that you don't always get what you want and that often life isn't very pretty."

Brandon swallowed. All that pain. Senseless and cruel. It hurt him that there was nothing he could do about it—not yet, anyway. "Do you know anything about him?"

"No." Veronique slipped her hand from his and dropped it to her lap. "Maman refuses to talk about him. I used to ask her all the time...on occasion I'd even begged her to, but she—" Veronique's eyes filled with tears suddenly, tears not for herself but for her mother. "You know, she hasn't been with a man since. Not even out on a casual date."

"I'm sorry," Brandon said, his voice tight. Fury welled in his chest. He was furious at his father's greed and old man Delacroix's narrow-minded bigotry. And with himself for his unwitting part in it. "I need to go," he said suddenly, pushing away from the table and standing. "Where can I drop you?"

Hurt left a bitter taste in her mouth. She'd just shared with him her innermost feelings, had shown him a part of herself others rarely saw. And he'd tossed it back at her. She wouldn't make that mistake again. "Nowhere." Veronique tipped back her head and smiled up at him. She thought her cheeks would crack with the effort. "I'm going to finish my drink, then catch the streetcar up to Maman's. Maybe I can talk her into a pizza." When Brandon hesitated, she said too brightly, "Go on, I'm fine."

He gazed down at her upturned face for long seconds, his expression hard and unreadable. He didn't smile; he didn't try to touch her. Veronique silently cursed her own need for him to do both. Finally he pulled his keys out of his pocket and said, "I'm sorry, but I'd forgotten...I'm meeting someone."

"No problem." She shrugged and popped a pretzel into her mouth. She almost choked on it.

Brandon jiggled the keys in his right hand. "I liked being with you this afternoon. It was—"

"Fun," she supplied casually.

Brandon drew his eyebrows together. "Yeah, fun." He jiggled the keys again. "See you around."

Veronique watched him walk away. She didn't take her eyes from him until he'd pulled the small, too fast car into traffic and disappeared. Her throat was dry, her pulse fast. She stared blindly down at her half-finished drink. When had it happened? When had being with Brandon become more than a lark? When had she crossed the line between friendship and affection? She'd broken one of her own rules: she'd let him get too close.

Her fingers curled around the damp glass. He could hurt her. The realization was terrifying. For years she'd cherished invulnerability and independence above all else. And now—now she had this burning need to be with another person, even if it meant losing a part of herself to him.

Her expression hardened as she thought of the Christmas morning when she was seven. She and her mother had still been living with Grandfather Jerome, and she remembered watching her cousins open their presents—a porcelain doll collection for Tina and Louise, a complete train set for Barry, a Newfoundland puppy to be shared by all three—and realizing that there weren't as many gifts for her and that hers were somehow not as big or important.

She remembered the feelings—jealousy, disappointment and a longing so poignant that her chest had hurt. She hadn't felt that way since she'd decided to stop living for other people's approval. Until now.

She tilted her chin defiantly and narrowed her eyes. She wouldn't allow herself to care for him; she couldn't chance the pain. She and Brandon were acquaintances and would be nothing more. Any feelings she had for him could be ignored. Or controlled. *Sure they could.*

Veronique left a tip on the table, dropped the rest of her change in her tote and stood. Her confident smile faded as she stared across at Uptown Finery's now-empty parking lot and wondered if he would call.

Seven

Veronique was awakened by a loud rapping. Groaning, she rolled onto her side and pulled the pillow over her head. The sound came again. Damn neighbors, she fumed, realizing she wasn't going to be able to get back to sleep. Didn't they know it was Saturday morning? She sat up in bed, pushed the hair out of her eyes and squinted at the clock. Eight-twelve—the middle of the night as far as she was concerned.

The rapping came again, and Veronique jumped. It wasn't her neighbors; there was someone at her front door! Whoever it was she would have their head. "I'm coming, I'm coming," she called, pushing away the covers and getting out of bed. She stomped toward the door, cursing under her breath the whole way.

She swung the door open; the indignant tirade died on her lips. It was Brandon. He looked wide awake, freshly pressed and way too appealing. The jerk. "What," she asked, making a great show of irritation, "do you want?"

Brandon's lips curved into a self-satisfied smile. He could spend a lifetime surprising her. "I like your pj's," he said, eyeing the oversize garments. "Cowboys, aren't they?"

"Dale Evans and Roy Rogers commemorative pajamas," she muttered, folding her arms across her chest. "You never answered my question."

"I brought breakfast." Her voice was still froggy with sleep; her hair was a tangle of whiskey-colored silk. Brandon decided she'd never looked more desirable. "Sausage-and-ham biscuits from Popeyes."

"Yeah?" She caught a whiff of the biscuits, and her mouth began to water. Popeyes, known for its spicy Cajun chicken, had the best biscuits in the South. "Got any coffee in there?" she asked grudgingly.

"I was depending on you to supply the coffee."

"You're pushing it, Rhodes." Veronique scowled, but stepped aside. "Instant's going to have to do."

He followed her to the kitchen. "Are you always surly in the morning, or did you have a bad night?"

She filled the teakettle with water, took the jar of coffee from the shelf and got out two cups. That done, she turned back toward him. "I like to sleep." She absently scratched her arm. "What's *your* story? Are you always this chipper in the morning, or are you only doing this just to bug me?" His smile was her answer, and she sagged against the counter, resting her chin on her fist. "I'm too sleepy to fight back."

He smiled. "That's like handing a killer a loaded gun."

The curving of his lips was slow and sexy. Veronique's toes curled. The man packed quite a punch. "A gentleman would have let that pass."

"True," Brandon murmured, his eyes lowering. In her bent position, her huge pajama top opened slightly, revealing the creamy swell of one breast. Desire was swift and stunning; his abdomen tightened with it. He wanted to peel away those silly garments and discover the woman beneath—discover her with his hands and mouth and tongue. His eyes returned to her. "But a gentleman wouldn't be standing here thinking about taking advantage of a semiconscious woman."

A thrill raced up her spine. "And are you?" Veronique asked, her voice sounding impossibly husky even to her own ears.

"Yes." He leaned toward her.

Her lips parted as she angled her head for his kiss. "I'm glad."

They both jumped as the kettle started to whistle. Brandon groaned and motioned for Veronique to stay where she was; he needed to do something with his hands.

Veronique smiled sleepily and watched him through half-lowered eyelids. The last thing on her mind should be making love to Brandon Rhodes. But that was *all* that was on her mind. When she closed her eyes images of them together— his hands on her body, hot and urgent, his weight pressing her into the mattress, his lips covering hers—played on the back of her eyelids.

It really was a shame, she told herself, yawning. She would have liked to make love to Brandon Rhodes, but even now, before the last of sleep's cobwebs had cleared from her brain, she knew it was impossible. They weren't meant for each other, and she had to protect herself.

Brandon turned, catching the dreamy expression. What was she thinking about? "Plates and napkins?" he asked.

Veronique straightened, stretched and yawned again. The smell of coffee was working its magic. "First shelf to the right of the sink and drawer to the left of the stove."

She helped him carry everything out onto her balcony. It overlooked St. Peter Street and was only big enough for an ice-cream-parlor-size table and two chairs.

"You're the only person I know who lives in the Quarter." He watched as she added three tablespoons of sugar and a more than generous amount of cream to her coffee.

"No wonder you don't care if you drink instant—that's a kiddie coffee."

"I don't doubt it," she murmured, referring to his comment about her choice of living arrangement and ignoring the one about her taste in coffee. She unwrapped a biscuit; her eyes met his. "As you very well know, you never answered my question. Why are you here?"

Brandon laughed. Direct and to the point. She never pulled any punches. If he were playing fair, he would afford her the same courtesy. He wasn't. "I thought we should get an early start."

"Oh? And where did you think we were going?"

With exaggerated nonchalance he took a sip of his coffee, then unwrapped a biscuit and took a huge bite. "I love these things," he said blandly. When she let out her breath in a long huff, he wiped his mouth with a bright yellow paper napkin, took another sip of coffee then said, "To find a photographer."

Veronique carefully set down her biscuit. Her gaze swept over him, and she thought for a second time that morning that he was too appealing. "Why are you doing this? Why yesterday—" she gestured at their breakfast "—why now?"

His gaze shifted to a point over her left shoulder for a moment before returning to hers. "Why does it matter?"

It matters because I'm starting to care for you, Veronique thought quickly. It matters because I can't allow you the opportunity to hurt me. But she didn't say any of those things. "Answering questions with questions?" she murmured, feigning coolness. "Tacky, Brandon."

"You started this game, Veronique," he said softly. "I'm just playing it out."

She pushed away the now-unappetizing breakfast and stood. Self-preservation, she reminded herself as her eyes met his. "You're right, I started the game, now I'm ending it. More coffee?" Without waiting for an answer, she collected the two still half-full cups and headed toward the kitchen.

Brandon jumped up and followed her. By the time he reached the kitchen, she was standing at the stove, her back to him as she stared at the teakettle. "What do you mean you're ending it?"

She looked over her shoulder at him. "I should think it's obvious. I fold, Brandon."

"I don't believe it," he drawled, leaning against the doorjamb and folding his arms across his chest. "Veronique, the woman who calls herself a chance taker and a gambler, is backing down from a challenge." He shook his head and made a clucking sound with his tongue.

Veronique whirled around. "If you were any kind of gambler, you'd know that folding is a strategy. The skilled player, the smart player knows when it's advantageous to fold."

Brandon laughed. "It seems to me that it doesn't take a lot of brains to know how to quit."

Her cheeks warmed with anger. "This is ridiculous. I refuse to—"

"You're quitting," Brandon interrupted, "because you know you can't win."

He was right—she knew this was a no-win situation. But she would never admit that to him. She lifted one shoulder in a casual, bored gesture. "The game's not fun anymore, Brandon. It's as simple as that."

A muscle jumped in his jaw. He pushed away from the door and crossed to her. "Sounds to me like you're running away," he murmured, stopping in front of her. He trailed a finger down her flushed cheek.

The casual gesture raised a flood of warm feelings and tingling sensations, and Veronique forced herself not to jerk her head away. The action would reveal more than she wanted to. Her gaze held his as she said, "I never run. You'd be wise to remember that." Only then did she step away from his touch. "I'll be ready in twenty minutes." The smile that snaked across his face made her blood boil. She whirled around and headed toward the bedroom.

True to her word, twenty minutes later she walked out onto the balcony. She was dressed as eccentrically as ever in black knit pedal pushers and a crop top, a black felt gaucho hat trimmed with pink ball tassels and, at her waist, a huge pink patent-leather belt.

Away from Brandon's disturbing presence, she'd had time to think and had come to the conclusion that if he wanted to continue this silly game, she might as well have some fun. After all, she specialized in silly games, and if she made a practice of anything, it was having fun. She would just be careful. Very careful, she thought as Brandon looked up at her and smiled.

"Interesting outfit," Brandon said. The bizarre getup was a foil for her tall, slim build and striking features, and he thought her the most exotically beautiful woman he'd ever known. His eyes swept over her, lingering on the sliver of smooth pale flesh at her midriff. His eyes, smoky with awareness, met hers. "But then, you have lots of interesting outfits."

Veronique's stomach flip-flopped. Damn those eyes of his. It ought to be illegal to have eyes as seductive as gray velvet, as inviting as a spring-fed pool. How was she supposed to be careful when his every glance sent her pulse racing and her mind wandering? "I'm flattered you noticed," she said after taking a deep steadying breath and leading him back into the living room. She closed the balcony door behind her, then fastened the dead bolt. "Do you have any photographers in mind?" she asked, turning back toward him. "Or are we just going to randomly waste someone's time?"

"Why don't you wait and see."

She shot him an amused look as she grabbed her oversize tote. "Not showing your hand. You're getting smart, Rhodes."

They laughed together and headed outside.

There wasn't much on-street parking available in the French Quarter, so they had to walk several blocks. Veronique didn't mind. It was a clear, brilliant day, and the exercise got her blood moving. As they walked, she lifted her face to the early morning sun, enjoying its warmth against her cheeks. She breathed deeply. The breeze carried the scents of baking bread, boiling seafood and spring flowers. Veronique smiled. She'd lived in the Quarter for six years; every morning was the same as the one before. It was the one area of her life in which she enjoyed predictability.

Although it wasn't even ten yet, the street was already bustling with activity. Vendors chatted with one another as they prepared for the Saturday crowds; a street musician, hat already at his feet, warmed up on guitar while his partner tap-danced to the tentative melody; delivery men hurried through their rounds, shouting orders or laughing over some bawdy joke. Veronique waved and called greetings to people as they passed—a woman sweeping the doorway of a shop, a portrait artist setting up for the day, a young man on roller skates.

"Do you know everyone?" Brandon asked as she stopped to pet a small red dog she called Pepper.

"Almost." She straightened. "That's why I like living in the Quarter. There's a sense of family and of neighborhood here. We all look out for each other; we all care. Uptown—" she paused to shout a hello to the Lucky Dog hotdog vendor "—you all live behind alarm systems and security gates. You nod cool greetings to one another only when courtesy demands it and gloat over each other's misfortunes."

Scars from living with Jerome, Brandon thought, glancing at her set expression. And from being on the receiving end of too much of the Lily St. Germaine brand of cruelty. "We're not all that way," he murmured.

"No," she said with a small toss of her head. "It grows in direct proportion with the uptowner's assets. The better the balance sheet, the bigger the bigot."

And with the scars came bitterness. What lengths would she go for revenge? The thought flitted through his head, and he pushed it away. "What about me, Veronique? My balance sheet looks pretty good."

Veronique sent him a long, thoughtful glance. After a moment she said, "You've surprised me, Rhodes. But I'm not committing."

She was a straight shooter, at times even brutally frank. Would a woman like that look for revenge? He suspected not, but he had to know. And to know he had to gain her trust. Ignoring the gnawing guilt, he laughed and draped an arm across her shoulders. "You're a hard woman, Veronique Delacroix."

"Yeah." Veronique's mood lightened, and she laughed with him. "Hard and nasty." They'd reached the Porsche. Brandon opened the passenger door for her, then went around to the other side. "Had enough of my driving for this century, have you?" she teased as he slid in beside her.

Brandon smiled and started the car. "Not at all. I just know where we're going."

"Right," Veronique muttered, leaning her head back against the headrest and closing her eyes. "Nudge me when we get there."

"Can I nudge you anywhere I want?"

Veronique shot him an amused glance. "You like to live dangerously."

Brandon reached across the seat and tapped the end of her nose. "That's your department, lady. I'm just an apprentice."

Veronique lowered her eyes. Nothing between them had changed since their first night together. He was still bored, and she was still a diversion. And that would never change, she sternly reminded herself.

They didn't speak again until Veronique realized that they'd driven out of the downtown area and that Brandon was headed for Slidell. "I hate to burst your bubble, but you're going to find more photographers that way." She jerked her thumb over her shoulder.

"I thought we'd stop for lunch first," he said easily.

Veronique lifted her eyebrows in surprise. The man was crazier than she was. "Okay, I'll bite. Why are we going to lunch at ten in the morning?"

"We're not." His tone was amused. "By the time we reach the Gulf coast, it'll be noon."

"The Mississippi Gulf coast?"

"Yeah. Ever heard of Mary Mahoney's?"

"No." She cleared her throat to hide a laugh. "What about the photographer?"

"A ruse to get you to go to lunch with me."

For a moment she sat in surprised silence. But for a moment only. Then her lips began to twitch, her eyes crinkled at the corners, and she started to laugh. "Don't think you're going to get out of this so easily. You promised me a photographer, and I'm going to hold you to it."

For the rest of the trip they talked easily, discussing Louisiana politics, swapping names of favorite Cajun restaurants, exchanging stories about previous visits to the coast. And as they did, Veronique fell more under Brandon's spell. He was charming, intelligent and insightful. She found herself noticing and admiring things about him she hadn't before: the way his lips curved right before he laughed and how that laugher softened his chiseled features, the way his thick dark hair curled at his collar and ears and that his was the most perfect nose in profile that she'd ever seen.

In what felt like no time at all she caught her first sight of the Gulf of Mexico. As it had everytime since she was a child, the shimmering expanse of blue took her breath away. And like the child of so many years ago, she stuck her head out the window and breathed in the damp salty air.

"If you'd like," Brandon said softly, touched by her rapt expression, "we can stop and take a walk."

"Yes," she murmured, not looking at him, not being able to tear her eyes from the picture in front of her. "Yes, I'd like that."

A short time later they stepped onto the sand and walked toward the water. It wasn't a pretty beach—the sand wasn't white and it was littered with bits of driftwood, hunks of seaweed and trash—but she loved it anyway. The seashore had always been her haven, a place where she could go to feel absolutely contented and at peace. Veronique glanced up at Brandon, thinking that it seemed somehow right that she should be sharing this special place with him.

They walked in companionable silence for several seconds. Veronique broke it first. "Listen," she whispered. "It's beach music."

The pink tassels on her hat swayed as she moved. Brandon found himself watching the play of light and shadow on her delicately-boned face. At first he didn't realize she'd spoken. "I'm sorry, what?"

"Beach music," Veronique repeated. They passed two little boys who were noisily building a sand castle. She smiled and said hello then looked back up at Brandon. "The sound of the water, the cry of the birds, the squeals of those children." Her expression softened. "We used to come here every summer," she continued, not expecting or waiting for a comment. "There's a picture of me playing tag with the waves." She laughed at the memory. "I was four and had on this bathing suit with ruffles across the seat."

"Sounds cute."

"Yeah, I was a cute kid."

They stopped at the point where dry sand became wet and stood looking out at the horizon. She stuffed her hands in her pockets and looked up at him. "I've always loved the water. Pools, lakes, the ocean—" laughter bubbled to her lips "—bath tubs. It makes no difference to me. Maman used to call me her little porpoise. I'd play for hours without tiring, then cry for hours after we went home. I used to wonder if..." Veronique's voice trailed off, and she looked back out at the Gulf. Several seconds passed before she said lamely, "Maman hates the water."

Brandon's breath caught. She looked so young and so vulnerable standing there facing that unforgiving expanse of blue and her own memories. He reached out and tucked a strand of her hair behind her ear. His fingers lingered there, tracing the ear's contour, finding the pulse that beat wildly behind the lobe. "What did you wonder?" he asked, although he already knew. For a second he thought she wouldn't answer, then her eyes met his almost defiantly.

"I wondered if my father also loved the water. I wondered if he was a strong swimmer, if he would have come to the beach with me and Maman and sat in the sun with us drinking lemonade and laughing." Her eyes filled, but she didn't look away.

"I'm sorry," Brandon whispered, touched by her strength. Cupping her face in his hands, he stroked her cheeks with his thumbs. He bent his head and tenderly brushed his lips over her eyelids, her forehead and, finally, her lips.

Veronique's chest tightened at the sheer sweetness of the gesture, and the tears that filled her eyes threatened to spill over. She wanted to throw herself into his arms and cling to him. She longed to cry out the fear and loneliness she'd felt so often when growing up. But to do so would be to fully expose herself, and she couldn't take that chance.

She willed away the tears and squared her shoulders. It took all her strength, but she stepped away from his comforting hands. "Why should you be sorry?" she asked, a catch in her voice. "You had no part in my past. This has nothing to do with you." The tears threatened to fall again, and she turned and started running back toward the car.

He felt like a heel; he felt like a fraud. He went after her anyway. He grabbed her arm and swung her back around. "Don't shut me out, Veronique." His voice lowered. "Trust me."

"I can't." Her voice was high and breathless.

"Trust me," he said again, drawing her toward him. Her hands splayed against his chest, her back arched, and her head fell back. The hat dropped to the sand.

This had nothing to do with gaining her trust, Brandon acknowledged, his eyes lowering to her mouth. This had to do with a hammering heart and swimming senses. It had to do with the scent of her hair and the taste of her lips. And it had to do with need, dark and desperate and insistent.

The need was mirrored in her eyes, just as urgent but with a trace of fear. Brandon knew it wasn't him she feared, but her own response to him. The pulse beat wildly in her throat. He pressed his lips there, lingering over the soft, fragrant flesh. His blood swam as she moaned and moved against him.

Veronique's eyes fluttered shut as his tongue made a damp path over her collarbone. The breath shuddered past her parted lips as he slipped his hands underneath her crop top to stroke her back. She knew this was madness, but she'd lived on madness before and thrived. It was insanity, but she'd been called crazy too many times to count. Despite their differences and her fears, she wanted him. She gripped his shoulders tightly, silently begging him to kiss her.

And he did. His mouth sought hers, racing over it hungrily. Veronique tangled her fingers in his hair, drawing him closer, deepening the kiss. Their tongues met, mated and retreated, then started the frenzied dance again.

She hadn't known passion could be like this. She'd thought it pleasant, nice. If passion was pleasant and love-making nice, then what was this absolute abandon, this maelstrom of sensation she was experiencing now? She felt as if she'd been shattered into a billion pieces, then put back together again—better, more whole, than before. A thread of panic wound through her as she realized she would never be the same.

Veronique stood on tiptoe and pressed her body to his. She felt his arousal in the heat of his body and the urgency of his hands, and her fingers tightened in his hair. His teeth scraped against her cheek as he dragged his mouth across to her ear. It was a moment before she realized he'd said something. Veronique made a sound of protest and tried to pull his mouth back to hers. When he resisted, her eyelids fluttered up. His gray eyes were stormy with need and checked desire, his breath short and ragged with passion. "Trust me," he murmured again, almost fiercely.

Veronique dropped her hands to his chest. His heart beat wildly under her palm, and she curled her fingers into the soft weave of his pullover. Comprehension was slow, insinuating itself into her drugged brain like smoke through the crack under a door. He wasn't asking for her body, she knew. He wanted something even more precious from her. She couldn't afford to give it to him, but was afraid she hadn't the strength to refuse. Her only defense was to move away from him now. She acknowledged the truth of that, drew a deep shuddering breath and stayed where she was.

Brandon held his body still as he gazed down at her face. Nothing about her had changed—her body was still nestled against his, warm, pliant and inviting; her lips, still damp from his tongue, were softly parted; her fingers still clung to him—but he'd lost part of her. He sensed her withdrawal as surely as if she'd shouted it, and he would settle for nothing less than everything.

Brandon wrapped a wisp of her hair around his index finger. It was soft and shiny, and he knew if he held it to his nose, he would catch the tang of lemon. He gave in to the urge, and the scent enveloped him. "Your hat fell off," he murmured finally.

"I know." Her eyes, glazed and hungry, never left his.

His fingers moved in lazy circles on her naked back; he wasn't aware of the movement. "We should go."

"Yes." Her tongue darted out to moisten her lips. "We'd better."

Brandon groaned and said more sharply than he'd intended, "Stop looking at me like that, Veronique. I'm trying to be a gentleman."

The last of passion's lethargy lifted, and Veronique's eyes cleared. She had no idea why he stopped; she only knew he had. She also knew she'd made a total fool of herself.

Veronique stepped away from him and bent down to retrieve her hat. She slapped it against her thigh to knock the sand off, then looked back up at him. "Didn't anyone ever tell you, Brandon, that nice guys finish last?" She turned and walked back to the car, aware of Brandon's eyes on her and of the exact moment he began to follow.

He caught her just as her senses registered the heat of the door handle. He planted himself behind her, placing a hand on either side of her head, trapping her between him and the car. There was nowhere she could go, so she turned to face him. A tremor moved up her spine at his furious expression, then she tilted her chin and met his gaze evenly. She arched one delicate eyebrow and moved her eyes over him impudently. "You wanted something?"

He wanted something all right, wanted so badly he hurt. And she knew it. "Don't push me, Veronique."

She splayed her hands against his chest and leaned toward him. "And what are you going to do if I . . . push?"

His gaze lowered to her mouth, then lazily dropped to her breasts, lingering there until her nipples hardened and she shifted uncomfortably. When he'd made his point, his eyes returned to hers. "I wasn't being nice. I was being selfish. Because when I have you, Veronique . . . it'll be all of you."

"I wouldn't be so sure," she flung back.

A muscle jumped in his jaw. "Another challenge?" he asked quietly. "You *do* like to live dangerously." He dropped his arms and went around the car.

The blood drained from her face. He was right—she'd challenged him, his masculinity. Like a petulant teenager, she'd lashed out at him when he'd ended the embrace. Because she hadn't wanted it to end, because she'd been so carried away with sensations that she'd forgotten all about who he was and who she was and being careful.

Veronique stubbed her toe into the sand. She deserved his anger; he deserved her gratitude—he'd saved her from herself. She stared out at the Gulf for one brief moment, then got into the car. The silence crackled between them. "I was wrong," she finally said, looking straight ahead because she wasn't sure she could look him straight in the eye.

"Yeah," he muttered, then under his breath added, "but so was I."

The sun was dipping in the west as the New Orleans skyline came into view. Veronique sneaked a peek at Brandon. They hadn't spoken much since leaving the beach. They'd gone to Mary Mahoney's—a restaurant fashioned to look like an Irish pub—for lunch and feasted on huge, juicy hamburgers, onion rings and cold beer. Even then they'd merely exchanged pleasantries. Yet their silence hadn't been uncomfortable or angry, Veronique mused, but rather one of two people lost in their own thoughts.

After lunch they'd wandered around the small beach community, stopping to browse through touristy shops. Veronique smiled to herself as she thought of the tacky painted starfish she'd bought to set on her kitchen window ledge and of Brandon's expression when she'd insisted on buying it. "It's been airbrushed, for God's sake," he'd said, laughter in his voice.

"And sprinkled with glitter." She handed the starfish to the shop's salesperson, then dug around in her tote for her wallet. "It makes a statement."

"An overpriced one," he whispered in her ear.

"Yeah? You could say the same thing about that car you drive."

"Okay, if you want to compare a Porsche and a trinket..."

The rest of the afternoon had slipped away, and now, as the city came into view, she realized she didn't want it to end. She released her breath in a small, unconscious sigh.

Brandon shot her a glance from the corners of his eyes. "A penny for your thoughts."

Veronique lazily tipped her head in his direction. "You'd be losing money."

His laugh was soft. He reached across the seat and laid his hand over hers. "I enjoyed today."

Veronique's gaze shifted from his profile to the hand covering hers. He was wearing a Cartier watch. The elegant timepiece suited him, she thought. As did forty-thousand-dollar cars and fine restaurants and women in minks. As airbrushed trinkets and glitter-sprinkled objects suited her. She pushed the unsettling thought away and smiled. "I did, too."

He laced his fingers with hers. "All of it, Veronique."

His meaning was clear, and the blood rushed to her head. She felt suddenly breathless, too warm and totally vulnerable. Knowing she should distance herself from him now, before it was too late, she curled her fingers around his. They were strong, warm and comforting. She remembered how they'd felt against her cheek, strong but as gentle as the touch of silk against skin, and she smiled. Her voice was husky as she murmured, "So did I."

They didn't speak again until Brandon double-parked in front of her apartment building. He made a move to get out of the car, but she motioned for him to stay where he was. "You'll get a ticket," she said, opening the door.

"Don't forget your starfish."

"Thanks." She stuffed the small brown bag into her purse. "Well..."

"Yeah, well." He drummed his fingers on the steering wheel. "Veronique, I—"

A horn blasted behind them. "I wanted to tell... I needed to talk—" The horn sound again, and Brandon softly swore. "Never mind. It wasn't important."

Veronique doubted the truth in that statement, but wasn't sure she wanted to hear what he had to say anyway. She suspected she wouldn't like it. "You'd better go," she said, hurrying out of the car. "See you around." She waved and stepped up onto the sidewalk.

He opened his mouth to say something, but another honk, followed by an angry shout, stopped him. With a final, frustrated glance in her direction, he shoved the car into gear and took off.

Veronique stood on the sidewalk, watching him until the car had disappeared around the corner. She frowned as she realized he hadn't asked to come up and she hadn't offered. Sighing, she turned and headed inside.

Eight

___

Veronique hung the apricot-colored dress on the back of her bedroom door. As she ran her index finger over the be-jeweled fabric, the rhinestones caught the light and winked at her. It was hard to believe, she thought, that four weeks had passed since she and Brandon had bought this dress.

Four weeks. It had been four weeks of fun, of crazi-ness . . . of Brandon. He'd dragged her to photographers; she'd retaliated by picking the one with the corniest poses. He'd insisted on checking out caterers—but only ones who made those little pastry swans. They'd looked at florists, discussed locations for a reception and turned their noses up at every invitation they saw. Veronique shook her head. It was ridiculous, really. They were spending all this time on a wedding that would never take place.

Veronique turned away from the dress, crossed to the bed and sank onto one corner. She sat there a moment, then as if she hadn't the strength to remain erect, flopped onto her back and stared up at the ceiling. A long narrow crack ran from one edge of the ceiling to the other. The light fixture, she noted, needed to be cleaned.

With a small sigh, her thoughts returned to Brandon. They'd spent a lot of time together; in fact, since their trip to the Gulf coast, she'd seen him almost every day. But every time he'd initiated a reason for them to be together, he'd used the original game as an excuse. Her chest tightened, and her palms grew damp. He was still using her as a way to escape his stuffy life . . . and she was still letting him.

Veronique groaned and plucked at the brightly patterned bedspread. And worse, for the last four weeks she'd lied to herself. So effectively that she'd almost convinced herself that she was going along with Brandon because she never backed down from a challenge. Veronique laughed without humor. That was bull—she'd played along with him because she wanted to be with him and because she'd grown to depend on seeing him. Her fingers curled into her palms. Good God, the truth of that scared the hell out of her. She'd never depended on anyone before; she'd been independent, a loner and a maverick. No one had been able to touch her because she hadn't cared enough to let them.

But now . . . She rolled onto her stomach and rested her chin on her hands. Damn Brandon Rhodes anyway. He'd insinuated himself so completely and so stealthily into her life that she didn't know how she'd survived without him. And that made him dangerous.

But every time she reminded herself of that fact, he did something that made her happy. Like leaving a particularly funny comic strip in her message box or, knowing her fondness for sweets, sending her a dozen Mr. Chippy's giant chocolate chip cookies.

Veronique sighed and rolled back over. The problem was that just being with him made her feel warm and wonderful inside. Like the other night. "What do you mean, 'who won the 1947 World Series?'" she'd demanded, craning her neck to see the card Brandon held. "How am I supposed to know that?'' When he'd only laughed and made noises that re-sembled game-show timers, she'd lowered her eyebrows ominously. "Stop that! I can't think with all that noise."

"Tough, Delacroix. Time's up. What's your answer?"

Veronique drummed her fingers against the game board for a moment, then widened her eyes in mock surprise. "My God, there's a jumper on the ledge across the street." When Brandon whipped around to look out the window, she grabbed the card from his hand. His oath of surprise and her shout of "the Yankees" were uttered at the same moment, as was the spontaneous laughter that followed.

Before she could run for it, he had her pinned to the rug. "Didn't anyone ever tell you that cheaters never prosper?"

"Oh?" She arched a delicate eyebrow; her pounding heart belied the cool gesture. "I won, didn't I?"

A slow, wicked smile snaked across his face. His gaze lowered to her mouth. "A matter of opinion, certainly." He wound his hands in her thick, soft hair. "But I think I won this game."

Veronique laughed. The sound was husky and, she knew, too inviting. "I was talking about Trivial Pursuit, Rhodes."

"I like my game better." Grasping her arms, he rolled over so she lay on top of him.

Awareness skidded up her spine. Veronique twined her fingers in his hair. One bare foot began slowly, rhythmi-cally stroking his. "I'm not going to budge," she mur-mured, her lips only inches from his. "How do you propose we solve this dilemma?"

"I could ask you another question." He brushed his mouth against hers, then caught her sultry bottom lip be-tween his teeth.

Veronique shuddered. His tongue dipped in to taste hers, and her eyes fluttered shut in pleasure. Brandon's lips trav-eled to her ear; he lightly ran his tongue along its contour. "Well, Veronique?"

"Okay, cowboy..." Her words trailed off seductively, and her eyes lowered to his mouth. "Give me your best shot..."

Irritated with her wandering thoughts, Veronique sat up and pushed the tangle of whiskey-colored hair out of her eyes. It seemed all she did lately was moon over Brandon. A dozen times a day she would catch herself staring into space with a silly smile pasted on her face. Annoying.

Veronique pulled her fingers through her hair, catching sight of her reflection in the dresser mirror as she did so. Large, almond-shaped eyes, a mouth that seemed too big for her face, high cheekbones and a small straight nose. Hers wasn't a pretty face; she wasn't cute. An interesting face, she thought. Even striking. She leaned toward the mirror, turning her head to the right, then left. She'd long ago stopped wishing for a turned up nose and cupid's bow mouth. No, what bothered her now was the dreamy expression in her eyes and the rosy flush that stained her cheeks.

Veronique scowled into the mirror. She absolutely was *not* in love with Brandon. So what if he was an endearing combination of a romantic, a realist and Clint Eastwood? "What would you do," he'd asked one night while they ate pizza, "if you suddenly had a lot of money?"

Veronique had laughed and shot him an amused glance from the corners of her eyes. "Where in the world did that come from?"

His gaze shifted to a point over her right shoulder, then returned to her eyes. "Nowhere, I just wondered. So..." He helped himself to another piece of the ten-topping pizza. "What would you do?"

"How much money are we talking about?"

"Oh—" he thoughtfully rubbed his jaw "—say a hundred thousand dollars."

She laughed again. "I would never have guessed you were such a dreamer. But if you insist—I'd do something wildly impractical and totally self-indulgent. Maybe buy a Ferrari and take a trip to China."

"You're kidding," he said with obvious concern. "You wouldn't invest it?"

"Nope. I'm not the investment type." She sipped her beer, then added, "It'd be gone in a year."

"Veronique, that's crazy..."

Looking stunned and genuinely concerned, Brandon had spent the next twenty minutes explaining the finer points and wisdom of investing. Laughing to herself, Veronique shook her head. So what if he continually surprised her, leaving her off balance and pleased that she was? So what? She felt many things for Brandon, but love wasn't one of them. She liked him, enjoyed his company...she would even admit to a little infatuation—and even more lust. But not love.

She stood and stretched. If she was jittery and flushed it was only...her eyes narrowed in thought...only in anticipation of tonight's bash, her cousin Missy's debut party. Sure, *that's* why she was excited. She would see her mother and...and her cousins and a lot of other people who bored her silly. Veronique's eyes returned to the apricot dress, and she laughed. She was such a good gambler, she was even starting to believe her own bluff—the truth was, the only reason she was going to this stupid party was because Brandon was going to be there.

Veronique stood and walked back to the outrageous dress. Tonight she would be like a peacock at a party of swans. Her lips tilted at the fanciful image, and with one final look at the dress, she turned and headed into the bathroom to shower.

The next hour and a half passed quickly as she bathed and dressed. The gown fit as well as she remembered, skimming lovingly over her subtle curves, hugging all her roundest places as she moved. She stepped into her shoes, then pulled on the opera-length gloves. Veronique turned this way and that in the full-length mirror, her lips curving as she did. She'd never looked lovelier. It was amazing she could look so good in such a tacky dress. She shook her head and wondered what that said about her character.

The cabbie arrived right on schedule. She grabbed her wrap and bag, then swung the door open. "Perfect timing, I—" The words died on her lips. The man at her door was wearing a chauffeur's uniform, complete with white gloves and a cap. "I don't suppose you're from Speedy Cab?"

He smiled broadly and tipped his hat. "Your car, Ms. Delacroix."

"My car?" Veronique repeated. "Who sent you?"

"Mr. Rhodes, madam. If you're ready?"

He'd done it again—left her breathless with surprise and pleasure. "Is Mr. Rhodes with you?" she asked, hating the husky quality in her voice. She cleared her throat. "I've already called a cab."

"No, madam, Mr. Rhodes sends his regrets. Luckily I intercepted your cab downstairs and informed him that his services were no longer required. May I help you with your wrap?"

Minutes later Veronique stepped onto the sidewalk in front of her building. The white Mercedes limousine was double-parked, and there was a line of annoyed motorists backed up behind the automobile. She shot them an apologetic look and hurried toward the car.

The chauffeur held the door open, and she stepped inside, making a small sound of pleasure as she did. There was a single white rose laying on the seat, and the car's interior was fragrant with its sweet scent. Smiling softly, she picked up the flower and held it to her nose. Its scent was heady, almost overpowering in its subtlety. She lightly trailed the blossom over her lips and cheek; the petals were as soft and inviting as velvet.

What was Brandon up to? she wondered. He'd mentioned he was attending this party; he'd said he hoped to see her there. How had he known she would go? And why hadn't he asked her to accompany him? With trembling fingers, she snapped the flower's stem in two and tucked the blossom into the deep vee of her bodice.

The trip from the French Quarter to Uptown took twenty minutes. As the Creole architecture of the French Quarter gave way first to the high rises of the business district, then the Victorians of Uptown, her anticipation turned to nerves. What would she say to Brandon when she saw him?

The limousine pulled up in front of the Courtland Hotel, and the uniformed doorman sprang forward, opening her door with flourish. Placing her trembling hand in his, she alighted from the car.

The Courtland was one of New Orleans's oldest and most beautiful hotels. Its atmosphere one of rarified elegance and wealth. The chandeliers in the lobby were Baccarat; the paintings throughout the hotel were English Romantic and included a Gainsborough. Although she preferred places like Jack's and The Hummingbird, the Courtland was as much a part of her past as the Delacroix mansion on St. Charles Avenue and the Catholic girls' school where she'd spent her days from kindergarten through high school. Veronique glanced around the opulent lobby; she'd attended countless debuts, wedding receptions and Carnival balls at this hotel . . . but she'd never been as excited to walk through these doors as she was tonight. Her heels sank into the plush Oriental rug as she headed toward the staircase.

"Veronique?"

She heard her mother's tentative greeting from behind her and whirled around. She'd walked right by her mother and grandfather. "Maman!" Veronique pressed her lips to her mother's cheek, then glanced at the stern-faced man standing beside her. "Grandfather." She didn't wait for his reply, but turned back to her mother. "I'm sorry, I didn't see you."

"That's all right, sweetie. Your grandfather wanted some air, so we were just taking a little stroll around the hotel."

As usual, Veronique thought with more than a trace of anger, her grandfather demanded and her mother made concessions.

"You look beautiful tonight, honey. Are you meeting someone?"

Veronique jerked her thoughts back to her mother. There was a definite gleam in those blue eyes, she thought. Had she seen her pull up in the limo? "No, Maman. How do you like my dress?"

"Disgraceful."

Veronique heard her grandfather's muttered comment and shot him a glance from the corners of her eyes. Rigid disapproval emanated from every pore. Veronique's glance slid back to her mother; she obviously hadn't heard the comment as she'd started talking about a dress she'd seen last week at a well-known boutique. Veronique decided she couldn't let the comment pass and with a wicked grin leaned over and kissed her grandfather's cool, dry cheek. "You know, it's always a treat seeing you, Pawpaw." He cringed at the use of the local—and in his opinion classless—term for grandfather, and her grin widened.

"I'm going for a drink," he said curtly, then turned on his heel and headed for the bar.

"Oh, dear." Marie's forehead knit with worry as she watched her father march across the lobby. "I'd better—"

"Don't be silly, you're coming up to the party with me," Veronique inserted crisply. She slipped her arm through her mother's and steered her toward the curving cypress staircase. As they started up, Veronique said, "We can only hope a drink will mellow him. Of course," she added mildly, "there's always the chance he'll drink himself into a stupor."

When Marie coughed to disguise her giggle, Veronique smiled. The sound was girlish and carefree. She liked making her mother laugh; she'd laughed too little in her life. Veronique's smile faded. Jerome Delacroix was a tyrant, and her mother had lived under his thumb all her life. Why, Veronique wondered as she had for years, didn't she stand up to him?

As they approached the ballroom's open doors, the noise of the party separated into distinct, familiar sounds. The bluesy tune the band was playing, the sound of clinking flatware and crystal, hushed conversations and sudden laughter. And with each step Veronique's pulse quickened and her palms inside her gloves grew damp.

She saw him the moment she walked through the door. He was standing with the mayor, his head was bent as he listened to something the other man was saying. His black hair gleamed in the soft light, and Veronique's fingers itched to thread through the soft, dark mass. As if he felt her scrutiny, he lifted his head, and their eyes met across the crowded room.

Heart pounding, mouth dry, she stared at him. He looked the same in evening clothes as in jeans, she thought, her eyes racing over him. And he would look the same in rags or nothing at all—strong, elegant and confident. He was a man whose appearance could intimidate, a man who had known the power of money all his life and looked the part. But when she gazed at him all she felt was warm and tingling and whole.

Oh, dear God. She squeezed her eyes shut in a brief moment of panic. She'd lied to herself again. She was head-over-heels, Katie-bar-the-door, that's-all-she-wrote in love with Brandon Rhodes. Warmth spread over her until she thought she must be glowing. It wasn't smart; it was reckless, but she loved him.

"Veronique, honey, is something wrong?"

She pulled her gaze from Brandon's to look down at her mother's concerned face. "No, nothing...I...need to talk to...excuse me, Maman."

Knowing she would end up hurt but not giving a damn, Veronique wound her way across the room. And as she did,

Brandon began moving toward her. She brushed by a woman who smelled as if she'd bathed in Patou 1000 and bumped into another wearing a silver taffeta dress. But her eyes never left his.

Within moments she reached him. Feeling awkward and uncertain of everything but her love, she clasped her hands in front of her and just gazed at him.

Brandon was the first to speak. "That's a great dress," he murmured, his lips curving into a smile.

Her answering smile was slow and soft. "My fiancé helped pick it out."

Brandon's eyes swept over her. "He has terrific taste. In clothes—" his voice lowered "—and women."

Head and senses swimming, she held his gaze. "I think so, too."

He reached out and touched the blossom tucked between her breasts, then stroked the curve of flesh it shielded. There was no difference between the two—both were as soft as velvet, as white as snow. He bent to catch the heady scent . . . and equally as fragrant.

His dark hair brushed against her collarbone. The sensation—like dandelion down against bare flesh—was unbelievably erotic, and Veronique caught her bottom lip between her teeth to keep from sighing with pleasure. Would making love to Brandon be like skydiving? she wondered. All heart-stopping free-fall? Or all adrenaline and nerves, like a winning streak of craps? As he lifted his head he blew a gentle path on her exposed skin, and her fingers curled onto her palms. It would be unforgettable—she was already on fire, and he'd barely touched her.

He drew her into his arms. Together they moved to the music, cutting through the throng until they were at the very center of the dance floor and shielded on all sides by the other dancers. Tipping her head, Veronique's eyes roamed over his features, enjoying the clean angles and dark beauty of his face.

"You got my message," Brandon murmured.

The feel of his body pressed so closely to hers as they danced made her ache for a more intimate bond—a bond of flesh and heat and shared passion. Her tongue darted out to moisten her suddenly dry lips. "There was no message," she said, her voice a husky whisper. "Only the flower."

He laughed and twirled her around. "The rose," he said, pressing his lips to her ear, "was the message."

There was a tingling at her wrists, her elbows and behind her knees; her senses swam with his words and the meanings behind them. Her head fell back. "Tell me," she whispered.

His fingers at the small of her back began moving in slow circles. "I was thinking of you—" he dipped his head so he could catch the scent of her hair "—of all the things you were...of what you reminded me of."

She smiled and rubbed her nose across his chin. As she did she caught the tang of some citrusy after-shave. "You think I'm a rose? Why?"

"Because of your thorns...and your softness." He toyed with the tips of her thick, soft hair. "Because you're a contradiction."

She laughed and arched her neck so her eyes could meet his. They were as soft and warm as the moisture that hangs above a lake at dawn, and Veronique knew she could lose herself in their depths. She probably already had. "What if I were a dessert?" she asked, her tone at once teasing and provocative.

He smiled at the thought. "Something subtly sweet and endlessly satisfying."

His smile, Veronique decided, could tempt an ascetic, could gentle a rabid beast. Its effect on her was even more dramatic. "And a color?" She stroked the lapel of his tuxedo; even through the layers of fabric she could feel the beat of his heart. She leaned down and pressed her lips to the place her fingers had just caressed.

He slowed his steps with the music, and they swayed together like lovers who'd been long separated and were now reunited. "Red. The color of life...and of heat."

His simple words were an aphrodisiac more powerful than a witch's brew, a moonlit night or anything else she'd ever known. The breath shuddered past her parted lips. "And if I were a dog...would I bite you?"

The music had stopped—Veronique noticed, but didn't care. People were staring—she felt their curious glances against her back, but ignored them. She acknowledged only a pounding heart and swimming senses; she understood nothing but need and heat.

"Never." He brushed his lips over hers. They were moist and slightly parted; his tongue dipped in to taste hers. "You'd be an exotic breed, independent but fiercely loyal."

She laughed lightly and slid her hands up to his shoulders. "Loyal only to you?"

"Mmm-hmm." He lowered his lips to taste hers again. He felt her shuddered exhalation and smiled. "You would belong to me...and I would be yours."

She curled her fingers around his shoulders, squeezing, lightly massaging. His words conjured all sorts of images—images of sultry summer nights and shared secrets, of midnight passions and morning pleasures.

He pressed his lips to the pulse beating wildly behind her ear. "What kind of dog would I be, Veronique?"

She didn't have to think; there was no other choice. "A Doberman. Dark, sleek and dangerous."

"Then we're in luck," he said softly. "Because you're a woman who likes danger, a woman who thrives on adventure, on taking risks. It's in your blood."

He was right. The ordinary, the easy, the safe was not for her. It never had been, it never would be. She was a chance taker and a gambler—and she was placing everything she had on a long shot. She would do it without looking back, without recriminations.

Veronique tipped her head coquettishly. Her saucy gaze met his. "Are you trying to seduce me?"

He smiled, pleased, as always, with her directness. He would be just as direct. "Yes."

The music had started again, and Veronique followed Brandon's lead. "Overconfidence leads to mistakes," she teased.

Brandon drew her closer into his arms. Together they moved to the music. "I know what I want, and I'm going after it."

Awareness was a living thing; need ballooned inside her. "I'm not going to make it easy for you," Veronique warned, not even blinking at the lie. She was such a fraud—she was already his.

"Oh? What will I have to do? This...?" He pressed his lips to her ear, then caught the sensitive lobe between his teeth and nipped. "Or this...?" He trailed his lips down the side of her throat, pausing now and again to taste with the tip of his tongue. "Or maybe this...?" His lips caught hers in a long, thorough kiss. When he lifted his head, he whispered, "Well, Veronique?"

His touch flowed over her like hot butter over popcorn; she succumbed to the sensation. Tilting her head, she laughed up at him. "Yes to all of it or any of it." She gripped his shoulders urgently. "Kiss me again."

He did. Lips joined, they twirled to the music, spinning through the startled guests. Moments became minutes, and after that time could be measured only in heartbeats and promises.

When the band stopped for a break, Veronique collapsed against Brandon's chest. "I feel drunk," she said, delightfully out of breath. "But I haven't had a drink."

"That's part of my plan."

"Then it's working." She pulled off a glove so she could thread her fingers through the soft black hair that brushed his collar, then with a quick laugh, tossed the glove over her shoulder. There were startled gasps, shocked glances. "We're scandalizing the blue bloods," Veronique whispered, standing on tiptoe so her lips were only a breath from his.

"Yeah," he murmured, liking the way her mouth hovered so near his, "but I don't give a damn."

"Oh?" Hands splayed against his chest, she leaned a little closer. "What are you going to do for an encore?"

"You wouldn't *believe* what I'm going to do," he said softly, running a finger down her flushed cheek. "To you..." The finger brushed lightly across her bottom lip. "With you."

Veronique's tongue followed his finger; she could taste him against her flesh. Her eyes met his. "Is this part of your seduction?"

He pressed more intimately to her. "When it starts," he murmured, "you won't have to ask."

Veronique's breath caught; desire was as stunning as a blow to her midsection. The pulse hammered in her head until she was light-headed with it. He was driving her mad with need. She'd never wanted anyone or anything with the ferocity that she wanted Brandon. And he knew exactly what he was doing to her.

"Thirsty?" he asked.

Her smile wasn't quite steady as she answered him. "Parched."

"I'll take care of that." He dropped a quick kiss on her lips. "Don't move."

How could she? Veronique wondered, watching as he moved through the crowd. She was as unsteady on her feet as she was light-headed. Her lips curved into a soft smile. She understood now why people afflicted with the malady couldn't eat, sleep or think clearly. With a small shake of her head, she lowered her eyes. Her glove was on the floor several feet in front of her; she crossed to it and bent to pick it up. There were heel marks on the delicate fabric, and she absently brushed them.

"Ms. Delacroix."

"Yes?" Veronique looked up.

One of the hotel's stewards smiled and held out a tray that carried a glass of champagne and a small ivory-colored envelope. "Mr. Rhodes asked me to deliver these."

"Thank you," she murmured, her eyebrows drawing together. Where was Brandon? She took the envelope and, as calmly as she could, ripped it open. Heat washed over her—tucked inside was a key. She nudged it with her forefinger. Engraved in an ornate script on the large oval tag was an *L* and an *A*. The Leona Alfonsi suite, Veronique realized. The most famous suite of rooms in New Orleans.

As she lifted her eyes, her gaze settled on her grandfather. He stood not a dozen feet away from her. His face was pinched and white; he stared at her fiercely. A sudden chill raced up her spine, and she clutched the envelope tightly. Why was he—

"Should I wait for a reply?" the steward asked, shifting impatiently.

Tearing her gaze from her grandfather's, she flashed the young man a smile. She took the champagne from the tray and downed it, then replaced the glass. "No, thanks. I can handle it myself." Unconsciously touching the rose at her breasts, she turned and headed toward the door. She didn't have to ask—the seduction had started.

Nine

The room was fragrant with the scent of roses. Heart thundering in her chest, Veronique closed the door behind her. For a moment she leaned against it, grateful for its support. Was she doing the right thing? She'd asked herself that question over and over during the ride up to the eighth floor. Being with Brandon felt right, felt wonderful, but her head warned her to be careful, and in truth, she was scared.

Veronique drew in a deep steadying breath. She wasn't a fickle woman: when she gave herself, she gave everything. Maybe that's why there'd been so few men—she hadn't been willing to share all of herself, the emotion hadn't been strong enough. But with Brandon she wanted to give and receive; she wanted to take and to share. She wanted it all.

There was an elaborate spray of white roses at the foot of the four-poster bed. Veronique pushed away from the door and crossed to the arrangement. A soft smile played at the corners of her mouth as she pulled one flower from the bunch. The thorns, she noted, had all been removed. She held the blossom to her nose, and her gaze circled the room. There was a champagne bucket and a serving cart beside an intimate table set for two. The antique globe lamps bathed the room in a warm golden light.

"Hi," Brandon said softly from behind her.

Veronique turned slowly. He hadn't surprised her—she'd sensed his presence before he'd spoken. "Hi," she echoed, her voice husky.

"I'm glad you came."

Veronique clasped her hands in front of her. "I'm not sure—" she cleared her throat "—it seemed so right downstairs...now..." Her eyes met his then skittered away. "Maybe I shouldn't have."

Brandon's chest tightened. He admired her honesty, but he didn't think he could bear for her to leave. If he pulled her into his arms now, she would melt against him. But he wanted her without reservations. He jammed his hands into his pockets. "Anything I can do to change your mind?"

Veronique lifted her gaze. The light was behind him as he stood in the doorway to the sitting room, and his silhouette was tall and broad against the rectangle of light. But there was an awkwardness in his stance: he looked stiff, uncomfortable and...nervous, she realized. He cared enough about her and her feelings to be nervous. Confidence surged through her; it would be all right—she was making the right choice, the *only* choice. "I think you already have."

Brandon's breath caught as her lips curved. Her smile was as seductive as a woman's could be; it held the promise of both passion and shadows. He knew that mouth would soften and part under his, but she was as much a mystery as an invitation. And it was her secrets that made him wait.

"The Leona Alfonsi suite," Veronique murmured almost to herself, glancing once again around the room. "New Orleans's most famous opera singer."

"Yes," Brandon said, his eyes never leaving her face. "She was also one of New Orleans's most colorful figures.

A true eccentric.'' He crossed to stand in front of her, but didn't touch her.

Veronique held the flower once more to her nose. The scent was at once earthy and ethereal. She breathed deeply and knew she would never be able to separate the scent of roses from a desire so strong she felt weak.

''She was a woman of passion,'' Brandon continued, bending his head to catch the blossom's scent, ''and conviction. A woman so filled with life that no one who met her remained unaffected by the experience.'' His voice lowered. ''Like you, Veronique.''

''You think so?'' She laughed lightly and stepped away. Two could play the seduction game. Knowing she would draw his gaze there, Veronique dropped the rose on the bed, then crossed to the window. She ran a finger along the edge of one of the lace curtains, then looked over her shoulder at him. ''She and Courtland were lovers...their affair was the most notorious of its day.''

Awareness tightened in his belly. Her eyes and voice were as sultry as an August night, and Brandon fought to control his body. ''It's said that Courtland promised to give her everything he had if she would stay with him.''

''But she didn't,'' Veronique said almost sadly. ''She couldn't.''

''Because she was fire,'' Brandon murmured, watching Veronique as she moved around the room. Her movements were liquid, lazy and sensual, and he was entranced by the gentle swing of her hips and the glitter of beads and rhinestones as they caught the light. ''And fire can't be contained or controlled.''

Veronique ran her hand along the polished front of the armoire, then stopped and looked at him. ''She knew he would never be hers. He was a Catholic and already married.'' How would she feel when Brandon married another? Veronique pushed the thought away and crossed to the champagne bucket. She pulled the bottle from its icy nest and examined the label. "Tattinger," she murmured. "Very nice."

What was she thinking? Brandon wondered, watching as she replaced the bottle then picked up a crystal ashtray and turned it over in her hands. She was the most elusive and exciting woman he'd ever known, and he wanted her with a greediness that shocked him. And with the greed came the fear that like the mercurial Alfonsi before her, she would never be his.

"They say—" Veronique replaced the ashtray and lifted one of the crystal wine flutes. She ran her fingers lightly over the delicate glass; she held it to the light. Without looking at him, she finished, "They say she haunts the hotel."

Setting down the glass, she crossed once again to the window. She moved aside the curtain and gazed down at St. Charles Avenue just as a streetcar lumbered past. "Would it surprise you if I said I believe in ghosts?"

Brandon cocked his head as he gazed at her back. Where was this heading? "No," he said softly, "it wouldn't surprise me."

Smiling to herself, Veronique let the curtain drop. He wouldn't believe in ghosts, she knew. Nor in magic, fairies or miracles. He was a man of reason and reality. But he understood who she was, and he believed in her. That was all that mattered. She turned back to him. "Champagne, please."

Silently Brandon crossed to the bucket and with easy movements popped the cork. He filled the two tall flutes with the effervescent wine and held one out to her.

As she took the glass from his hand, their fingers brushed. There was something intimate, something warm about the accidental touch, and Veronique's pulse fluttered. She lifted the glass. "What shall we drink to?"

"I would think that's obvious, Veronique," he said softly, and tapped his glass against hers. "To tonight."

Her heart skipped a beat. Those two words promised a passion few ever experienced and a heat most only dream of. She wished she could believe it was more than passion and that he, like Courtland before him, would give it all away for love. But she'd known the odds before she'd come upstairs, and they hadn't changed. Veronique lifted the glass to her lips; the wine was ice-cold and bracing as it slipped down her throat.

Seconds passed. The silence between them was almost too potent, and Veronique lowered her gaze to the serving cart. There were chocolates—Swiss, she decided, eyeing their dark, glossy surfaces—caviar, plump red strawberries, a variety of cheeses, crackers and breads. Her lips curved into a wicked smile. "This is an awfully well-planned seduction." She dipped her finger into the caviar, then stuck it in her mouth, slowly sucking the delicacy off. Her eyes never left his. "How did you know I would come?"

Arousal was instant, overpowering. He drew a sharp breath, then exhaled slowly. "I took my chances."

"I like a man who takes chances," Veronique murmured, picking out a small, dark chocolate. She held it to her lips, running her tongue experimentally along its rounded edge. His gaze hungrily followed her tongue as she tasted the chocolate, and she smiled ever so slightly. She felt like a temptress; the sensation was headier than the wine, more delicious than the chocolate. It was a sensation she could become addicted to. "But more—" her tongue darted out to taste the candy once again "—I like a man who takes liberties." Slowly, deliberately, she placed the chocolate on her tongue.

It took a moment for her words to register, but when they did, heat rushed over him in a fury. She wanted him without reservations; there would be no regrets. With a groan, he pulled her into his arms. And as he knew she would, she melted against him.

For a moment it was enough to feel her soft curves pressed against him, to gaze into eyes the color of heated honey, to catch her own subtle scent as it blended with the perfume of the flower between her breasts. But for a moment only. Contentment became hunger, and hunger raged out of control. Brandon's lips caught hers; they were soft, moist, already parted. Their tongues met, and a second after he smelled the chocolate, he tasted it. With a sensual shock, he realized she'd passed the melting confection from her mouth to his. With a sound of pleasure he accepted the gift. Its sweet, rich flavor flowed over his tongue, and he savored it. When he'd had his fill, he passed it back.

Veronique wound her fingers in his hair as she sucked the chocolate from his tongue. Did the candy taste the same to him as it did to her? she wondered dizzily. Sweet, dangerous and delicious? And what of her body pressed against his? Did it feel as achingly right as his did against hers? The last of the confection slipped down her throat, but the flavor lingered, and again she shared it with him, teasing and caressing his tongue with hers.

Veronique moaned as his hands moved down her back to cup and caress her soft swells, as he pressed her more intimately to him. She followed his lead, running her hands underneath his jacket to stroke his back and sides. Through the fine cotton shirt she felt the heat of his leanly muscled flesh—it was as if he were on fire.

She wanted that fire, she wanted to step into it, for it to surround her, consume her. "No more barriers," she rasped, pushing at his jacket. "I need to feel you against me. Now."

At her words, passion exploded between them. Gone was the capability for soft words and lingering caresses. This was as reckless as forbidden love, as steamy as an illicit rendezvous. He yanked off his tie while she worked at his shirt buttons. Under her urgent fingers, the fabric groaned, then gave, threads resisted, then snapped. He unzipped her dress; it slithered to the floor in a sparkling apricot heap.

His shirt followed her dress; hose and shoes were removed and kicked aside. Murmuring her need, Veronique pulled him to the bed. His body felt wonderful against hers, and she promised herself she would take time to linger over every nuance later. *Much later,* she thought as he captured the tip of one breast with his lips, then the other.

Veronique wound her fingers in his thick, black hair as he pressed kisses over her stomach, as his tongue dipped into her navel, then moved lower to taste, tease, kindle. She arched as his fingers, then his lips, found her, and she cried out when the sensations became unbearable in their sweetness.

Brandon moved back up her body until his mouth caught her strangled sounds of pleasure. Veronique smoothed her hands over his damp back, lightly scratching, absorbing his heat through her palms.

"Make love to me," she whispered. "I need you." As the words shuddered past her lips, she wrapped her legs around him.

Groaning, Brandon took what she offered, slipping slowly inside her. Their eyes locked, and for a long moment Brandon just looked at her. Her cheeks were wild with color, her eyes stormy with arousal. She was the most perfect woman he had ever known; she was the only woman who had ever really touched him. An ache that had nothing to do with passion and everything to do with need ballooned inside him.

He caught her mouth; their fingers laced. They rocked together, slowly at first, building speed until pulses hammered and skin was slick. Veronique cried his name at the same moment hers touched his lips. Gasping for breath, they hurtled together into the stratosphere.

The trip back to Earth was slower. Veronique explored his body with feather-light caresses of fingers and lips; it was taut and smooth, an enticing combination of rounded planes and gentle angles. He was beautiful, she thought, nestling against him. And for now, he was hers.

Brandon whispered soft words in Veronique's hair as he stroked the tangled, shiny mass. He smiled to himself as she murmured her contentment and curled into his side. He'd thought all along this was his seduction. He'd been wrong. She'd seduced him from the first—with her laughter, her honesty, her joie de vivre.

And somewhere along the line, because of her, he'd forgotten he was dissatisfied with life. No, Brandon corrected, looking down at her soft expression. He hadn't forgotten—he wasn't any more. Since meeting Veronique his life had become full and rich, filled with light and laughter.

Veronique trailed her tongue along his collarbone. His skin was warm and salty. Enjoying the combination, she tasted again, then moved on to another equally inviting spot.

"Good?" Brandon asked, amused.

"Mmm-hmm." She propped herself on an elbow so she could see his face. He looked sleepy and satisfied. She walked her fingers up his chest. "Yummy."

He ran the flat of his hand over the smooth curve of her hip. Tempting. He smiled as he realized they would make love again tonight—at least once—and that he was already wanting. "Hungry?"

"Uh-huh..." Veronique wiggled her toes against his. "What do you have?"

"Whatever you want."

When he leered at her, she pinched him in a place that had probably never seen the sun—at least not in New Orleans—then grinned as he cursed under his breath and rubbed the spot. "Witch."

Laughing at his expression, Veronique sat up and pushed the tangle of hair out of her eyes. "I've been called worse. Rowdy, hoyden, illegitimate brat. Once, Grandfather called me..." Noting his stillness, her words trailed off. It was as if she'd lost him. He was staring at a point somewhere behind her, his expression faraway and too serious. As she watched, his forehead creased, and his mouth, which moments before had been soft with pleasure, hardened. She wrapped her arms around her legs and rested her chin on her knees. He looked sad, Veronique thought at the same moment she realized it wasn't the first time she'd seen the look.

Needing to comfort him, she reached across and lightly touched his arm. "Brandon?"

With a small shake of his head, his gaze shifted to hers. He looked almost surprised at her serious expression. "What's up?"

Veronique shook her head, her silky hair rippling with the movement. "If you need to talk..." She looked away, then back. "You haven't mentioned your father in a long time... and I just wondered, well, if you were doing okay."

Brandon blanched. He'd been thinking about his father all right—about his father and her father. And his own dishonesty. *Tell her now,* he thought. Tell her now, while she's warm and lazy from spent passion. He took a deep breath, then let it out in a long silent sigh. Not tonight. There would be time tomorrow or the day after for a scene; tonight was too perfect to ruin with past hurts and present lies. "I'm fine," he said finally, and forced a smile.

"Oh." He didn't want to share his thoughts with her, she realized and couldn't quite hide her disappointment. She plucked at the satin coverlet. "Great. I'm glad."

Feeling like a cad, Brandon leaned over and kissed her. It wasn't great—he'd hurt her. And would again, he thought. "I was thinking about the Dallas store, that's all. You know, it takes a little time to adjust to being Mr. Big." When she smiled, he kissed her again. "Want me to bring the cart over?"

Relieved, Veronique smiled. "Mmm, and the champagne, too. No sense letting all the goodies go to waste."

"Don't worry," Brandon said, his eyes roaming slowly over her. "I haven't been." She wasn't the type to blush, so when she did it was that much more charming. He laughed and patted her heated cheek. "That particular shade of red is very becoming. You should wear it often."

"Think you can make me?" she asked, wiggling her eyebrows.

"Hold that thought," he murmured, then slipped naked out of bed.

Sitting cross-legged on the rumpled bedding, Veronique watched as he rolled the cart over, then went back for the champagne. He was gorgeous. Especially his rear, she thought with a wicked grin.

"What are you smiling about?" Brandon asked, eyeing her suspiciously. "You look like the proverbial cat with a canary."

Veronique laughed and scooted a little to the right to make room for him on the bed. "I was admiring a certain part of your anatomy." She made a sound that was a cross between a purr and a growl.

He handed her a flute of champagne, then sat next to her. "Make that sound again and you won't have time to drink that."

"Promises, promises," Veronique said as she perused the selections on the cart. "Are these chocolate-covered cherries?" She held up a dome-shaped candy.

"Mmm-hmm..." Brandon sat a little behind her, balancing the glass of wine on a knee and running his fingers lightly down her spine. "Speaking of parts of the anatomy..." he murmured, pressing his lips between her shoulder blades "...you've got a great back."

"Thanks." She glanced over her shoulder at him, her expression deliberately naughty. "You can kiss it again if you like."

"Oh, I can?"

"Yes, please." Laughter lurked in her eyes. "Do you like cherries?"

"Uh-huh." He placed a row of leisurely, open-mouthed kisses along her shoulders.

"Good." She bit the corner off one of the fruit-filled candies, then carefully sucked out its liquid center. The cherry was last, and she caught it on the end of her tongue. Turning, she pressed her mouth to his and passed him the cherry.

With a murmur of pleasure, he took it from her. He bit into the round fruit. It tasted as much of her as of the sugar, and Brandon eagerly accepted another. And another. As the last candy slipped down his throat, he dipped two fingers into the caviar and held them out to her. "Fish eggs?"

"Mmm-hmm...." Veronique laughed, then drew his fingers into her mouth, sucking the salty delicacy, teasing him by refusing to let go when they were clean.

Next, Brandon plucked the fattest strawberry from the bowl and held it to her lips. She slowly sank her teeth into the succulent fruit, letting the juices pool on her lips until they were wet and red. She moaned with pleasure and took another bite, nipping at his fingers as she did. The fruit's heady fragrance surrounded her as she fed and was fed.

When they'd devoured all, Brandon touched his finger to her mouth. It was red from the fruit and swollen from their passion. "Your lips are sticky," he murmured, his voice almost harsh with need.

Veronique caught the finger between her teeth and bit lightly. "So are my hands." She splayed them across his furred chest. "What are you going to do about it?"

His answering laugh was husky. "This..." He brought first one hand to his lips, then the other, placing lingering kisses in each palm. "And this..." He pulled one finger slowly into his mouth, his tongue moving over it, sucking it clean. Then he drew in another and another.

The sensation was incredibly erotic. Veronique curled her fingers around his face as his tongue drew designs on the sensitive flesh of her palm. She wanted him so badly she ached.

When she whimpered and tried to arch against him, Brandon pushed her back until she was sprawled on the bed. She was unbelievably sexy with her tousled hair and passion-flushed features, Brandon thought, his control beginning to snap. "More champagne?" he asked, his voice sounding harsh even to his own ears.

"Mmm..." She looked at him through half-lowered eyelids and smiled. "Do you think it'll revive me?"

Brandon's lips curved wickedly, and he trailed a finger over her breasts. Their peaks hardened in response. "I could ensure it."

"Oh, yeah?" Knowing it would drive him crazy, she stretched sinuously. When his eyes darkened, she laughed softly at her power. "That sounds like a dare."

"I've heard you never turn down a dare." He leaned over and placed a kiss on the inside of her thigh.

"True." Veronique sighed as he trailed his tongue up to the top of her thigh; her eyes fluttered shut as he tasted her most secret place.

Her flavor was more exquisite than any they'd just sampled, and he lingered over it, enjoying her throaty sounds of pleasure and the way her skin quivered under his tongue as he did. "Prepare yourself, Veronique."

His softly spoken words were her only warning. She gasped and arched as icy drops hit her belly and breast. Her eyes few open. The champagne pooled in her navel and slid over her sides. Just as a fine layer of chill bumps raced over her, he bent his head and lapped the sparkling liquid from her body. Soon, chill was replaced by heat, and she moaned.

"Sufficiently revived?" Brandon asked, his control slipping.

Head and senses swimming, Veronique looked at him. He was poised above her, his face and body rigid. She felt a moment of panic for tomorrow, then pushed it away. She loved him. She wanted him to fill her now, to be with her forever. Veronique opened her arms, and with a groan, he sank into her.

This time the joining of their bodies was less urgent. Gone was the frenzy that had made them rush, that had made them miss treasures found only through a thorough search. It was replaced by something softer, something solid. Veronique reached for him, but instead of clutching, she squeezed, stroked, pleasured.

She offered him her mouth; Brandon took it. How could it be that every time he kissed her she tasted sweeter? he wondered. And was it his imagination that with each kiss his need for another grew? He knew it was not and deepened the kiss.

Veronique wrapped her fingers in his hair, tightening her hold on him, bringing him even closer. In an imitation of their lovemaking, their tongues twined and retreated in an ancient dance. The dance started slowly, rhythmically, but built to a fever pitch, a point where reason was lost and reality was ecstasy.

As they reached that point and crested it, Veronique cried out and arched against him. And Brandon was there, holding her, calling her name, promising to stay. Then it was over, and as they'd shared the summit, they shared the descent, drifting slowly, inevitably back to Earth.

When their flesh had cooled and their breathing evened, Brandon started to pull away.

"No," Veronique murmured, her voice sleepy, lethargic. "Don't move. I want to fall asleep with you inside me."

"I'll crush you," he whispered, tenderly kissing the tip of her nose.

"I don't care."

"I do." Cradling her in his arms, he rolled onto his side so they faced each other, still joined. "Better?"

"It couldn't get any better," she said, yawning. "I'm so tired, but I don't want to let go of tonight."

"Don't worry," he said, smiling as her eyes fluttered shut, "there'll be plenty of time for us when you wake up."

Hours later, Brandon watched Veronique as she slept. She looked young and vulnerable, not at all like the daring adventuress she was. And not at all like the temptress who'd brought him beyond reason, again and again.

He reached down and captured several strands of her silky hair between his fingers. He'd felt like a rat when she'd asked about his grief and his feelings for his father. What could he have said? That the pain of his father's death had been replaced by something even more cutting—the pain of betrayal? Hardly.

A dozen times before tonight he'd tried to tell her what he'd learned, but every time something had stopped him. Guilt? Worry over her reaction? Cowardice? Probably all three, Brandon admitted, with a sigh.

So what now? He trailed his fingers over the curve of her shoulder; it was warm, smooth and tempting. He leaned down and placed a kiss where his fingers had just been, and she whimpered and snuggled more closely into his side. He had the unsettling feeling that he'd made a mistake, that he should have told her long ago.

Brandon shook his head and slid farther under the covers. Wrapping his arms around her, he nestled her back into the curve of his body. How could it backfire on him? No one knew the truth but him and Sebastian. Everyone else was either dead or only knew part of the story.

Brandon yawned. The thought of Sebastian telling Veronique was ludicrous. In truth, the lawyer would be happier if *no one* knew the story. Sebastian had even called last week to try to convince him to keep quiet. And as he'd explained to the attorney, he had to tell Veronique. But he had plenty of time. Sure. He was worried over nothing. He smiled in contentment as he drifted off to sleep.

Sunlight streamed across the bed. Veronique's lids fluttered up, and she moaned at the sting of light. Brandon was standing by the window, his expression thoughtful as he stared out at the day. "Hi." She struggled with the covers as she tried to sit up.

Brandon turned at her greeting. Her voice was raspy from sleep—or not enough of it—and her hair was sticking out in about fifteen different directions. His eyes crinkled at the corners; he was crazy about her. "Good morning."

She made sure the blankets were secure at her breasts. As she did, one corner of her mouth lifted in wry amusement. After last night the thought of modesty was ludicrous. "What time is it?"

"Early...about eight. Want some coffee?"

"Thanks." She placed a pillow behind her back, then scooted up a little more. "Do you remember how I take it?"

"Yeah." His smile was easy as he headed toward her. "Kiddie coffee. Right?" He handed her the cup.

"Right." She held the cup to her lips and sipped. The coffee was hot, sweet and bracing. And right now she needed bracing. She felt so awkward—like a gawky teenager around a group of polished college kids. So much for the legend, she thought as she took another taste of the coffee. The daring Veronique Delacroix was only brave when she had nothing to lose. And today she felt as if she had everything to lose.

"How is it?" He sat on the edge of the bed.

Her gaze jerked back to his. "Perfect."

He leaned down and brushed his lips against hers. They were warm and tasted of coffee. "No regrets?"

She smiled at the question. "No."

"I'm glad." He knew she was too honest to lie and returned her smile. "Spend the day with me."

Disappointment flittered across her features. "Can't," she said softly. "I promised Maman I'd come for lunch."

"Later then?"

Her cheeks warmed with pleasure. "Yes."

"Do you have time for breakfast?"

Veronique glanced at the bedside clock and felt frustrated. "No. I told her eleven-thirty, and I still have to go home and change." She winced as she thought of the apricot gown.

Brandon kissed her again, then stood up. "Wait here. I have a surprise for you."

Veronique watched him cross the room to the closet. A surprise? Moments later he placed a large box on her lap. She stared at it a moment, then met his eyes. "What's this?"

"For you." When she paused, he said, "Aren't you even curious?"

Veronique laughed and yanked the lid off. "You bet. I love presents." She peeled away the layer of tissue, then blinked in surprise. In this situation she would have expected lingerie or perfume, but a bright red sweater, matching stretch pants and a pair of red sneakers? She wasn't sure what to say or how to respond. Where were the quick wit and snappy comebacks she relied on so often? Why couldn't she think of anything to do but throw her arms around him?

"I hope it's wild enough. I didn't quite know where to go to find something you'd like." When she didn't comment, he prompted. "You *do* like it?"

"Yes. Very much." She held the sweater up. It was oversize and made of loosely woven cotton; the boat neck, she was certain, was made to fall off one shoulder. She curled her fingers into the soft, nubby fabric. "Why..." She cleared her throat; she couldn't meet his gaze. "Why did you do this?"

Brandon reached out and tucked her hair behind her ear. His fingers lingered there, lightly stroking the smooth, warm flesh. "I didn't want you to have to go out wearing last night's dress."

Veronique's eyes filled. Her mother was the only one who'd ever treated her as if she were special. And now he was doing it, and all she could do was cry. "How did you know my size?" she finally asked, her voice thick with tears.

"I called Mimi," he answered simply.

Love washed over her. It was a small thing; it had taken him only minutes to make the call. She'd never realized before how true the cliché "it's the thought that counts" was. He cared enough for her to think ahead, to worry about her feelings, her reputation. And it meant the world to her.

Brandon stood and held out his hand. "Do you have time for a shower?"

"Yes," she murmured, and threw back the covers.

Ten

Brandon loved her. Veronique took one last look at the hotel before stepping into the cab. She knew it, even if he didn't. What they'd shared had been so much more than passion. There'd been something permanent, something possessive about the way he'd looked at her and the way he'd touched her.

Veronique leaned her head back and closed her eyes. The last time they made love—she shivered as she remembered—he'd handled her tenderly, as if she were made of the finest porcelain. And lovingly, as if she were the most important person in the world. He loved her, she thought again, smiling to herself. Now all he had to do was realize it.

Shaking her head, Veronique glanced out the window of the cab. It went against everything she'd learned growing up, but she actually thought there was a chance for them. It seemed too much to hope for, and yet...and yet she couldn't help believing their relationship would work. She laughed out loud and saw the cabbie look at her in the mirror. She didn't care if he thought she was a lunatic; she felt wonderful, felt for the first time in her life as if everything was going her way.

Nothing could burst her bubble today, Veronique thought as the cab pulled to a stop in front of her mother's house. Giving the driver a too-generous tip and a brilliant smile, she alighted from the cab and ran up the steps.

Her smile died as the door opened. "Grandfather," she said, trying to hide her dismay. Her eyes slid to her mother. She was standing behind him and looked tense despite her sunny smile. Today, Veronique decided resolutely, even her grandfather couldn't spoil her mood. "Maman," she murmured, brushing past him to embrace her.

"Hello, sweetie. You look radiant."

Heat crept up Veronique's cheeks at both the speculative look the older woman slanted her and the thought that maybe her mother had seen her leave the ballroom last night and had known why. "And you're as lovely as always, Maman." She turned toward Jerome. "And what do we owe this visit to, Pawpaw?"

There was no way he could miss the defiant tilt of her chin or the challenge in her eyes. Veronique felt satisfaction as his eyes flicked over her, then narrowed. "I would think you'd show your grandfather more respect," he said, his tone brusque.

Veronique delivered him her haughtiest look. "Why? You never show me—"

"I heard Winnie ring," Marie interrupted, relief coloring her tone. "Lunch is on the patio. Shall we?"

Without a glance at her grandfather Veronique slipped her arm through Marie's, and they started toward the patio. "What's he doing here?" Veronique asked, her voice barely a whisper.

"He just showed up," Marie whispered back. "I can't imagine why. He knew we were having lunch together."

"We'll make the best of it," Veronique said, lightly squeezing her arm. "So, what's new, Maman?"

Her mother's smile was almost sly. "I could ask you the same question, and I suspect your answer would be much more interesting." When Veronique blushed, she patted her hand. "I won't push."

Thank you, Veronique thought. It was too soon to share her feelings with anyone. First she had to be sure of Brandon. But when she was, her mother would be the first to know.

They took their seats at the rectangular wrought-iron table, and Veronique was surprised when her grandfather chose to sit directly across from her. He usually avoided any seat where he would be forced to look directly at her. Today he was staring at her, his expression almost fierce. When he caught her quizzical glance, his features smoothed into a neutral mask.

The first part of the meal passed uneventfully except for the fact her grandfather never took his eyes off her. He watched her as if she were about to pull a knife or make off with the family fortune. What was he up to? she wondered not for the first time. When she was growing up, he'd either belittled or ignored her; this ceaseless scrutiny was both unexpected and disconcerting.

When he suddenly spoke, she almost choked on her last spoonful of cream of leek soup.

"How's everything in *your* little world, Veronique?"

He stressed the "your," and her mother's spoon clattered against the bowl. "Now, Father, you know Veronique is part of our world."

"Oh?" He patted his mouth with the linen napkin. "Is that true, Veronique? Do I belong in your world?"

Veronique's fingers curled into her palms, and she dropped her hands to her lap. She should have known better than to expect him to pass up an opportunity to needle her. But she wouldn't let him get to her. He'd long since lost the ability. "No," she returned evenly, "you wouldn't fit into my world."

"You see, Marie." He paused as Winnie whisked away the soup bowls then deposited plates of seafood crepes in their place. "Veronique understands what I mean."

She understood all right—he was leading up to something; she just hadn't figured out what yet. One thing she knew about her grandfather, he never did anything without a reason.

"So, Veronique..." He paused to taste his crepe, then murmured his approval before continuing. "Are you going to answer the question?"

She tipped her chin ever so slightly. "Why the sudden interest? Did somebody die and leave me money? Or have you lost all yours in the market and need to borrow some?" He flushed, and Veronique smiled in satisfaction. Victory was short-lived as, from the corners of her eyes, Veronique saw her mother wring her napkin in dismay. She was like a small distraught bird, and as she had all her life, Veronique felt the urge to protect her. If that meant biting her tongue, so be it.

"You know, Veronique," the old man murmured, seeming to change the subject, "your cousin Michelle is getting married. Peter Vincent...do you remember him?"

All thoughts of being quiet or anything else flew from her mind, and Veronique paled. Of course she remembered him, and her grandfather knew it. Peter Vincent was the first boy she'd ever loved—she'd chased him unmercifully, only to have him laugh in her face. "Why would I have anything to do with an illegitimate outcast?" he had asked. "A nobody?" She dragged her thoughts from the past when her grandfather spoke again.

"Everything is as it should be, don't you think? They are perfect for each other—similar backgrounds, education, goals—"

"Portfolios," Veronique inserted caustically, regretting her outburst the moment she'd uttered it. He would see it as a sign of weakness, and he would be right.

A ghost of a smile touched his lips. "That's part of it, of course. But they have the most important thing in common—a flawless bloodline. That's the unbreakable bond, a bond that represents the future."

Veronique's chest tightened until it was difficult to breathe. She wanted to tell him to go to hell. She wanted to tell him his bigoted, elitist attitude didn't wash in the eighties and that Brandon was different. But she couldn't because she wasn't sure she believed it herself. Her earlier elation and confidence seemed ludicrous now.

Her eyes filled with tears, and she tossed her napkin on the table. "Excuse me, I'll see if Winnie will bring us more tea." It took all her control to keep her head held high and her spine straight as she crossed the patio. Once through the door and just out of sight, she sagged against the wall.

How could she have let him get to her? Veronique wondered, squeezing her eyes shut and holding back the tears. And why did he have to be right? She'd been a fool to believe there was a chance for her and Brandon. Hadn't her own experiences taught her that wealth—

Her thoughts were interrupted by the crack of flatware hitting china, followed by an angry exclamation. That was her mother, Veronique realized in surprise. Concerned, she made a move to go back out onto the patio, stopping when she heard her own name.

"I want you to leave Veronique alone," her mother snapped.

"I'm only making conversation," her grandfather responded mildly. "It's what civilized people do."

"There's nothing civilized about what you're doing." Marie cast a quick glance toward the doorway, then turned back to him. "Don't bother lying to me. I know exactly what you're up to—you're trying to drive a wedge between Veronique and Brandon.''

Jerome patted his vest pockets. "It seems I've left my cigarettes in the living room. Excuse me."

Flushing, Marie grabbed his arm. "Don't you dare ignore me! I want to know why."

He looked at her for a moment, then sighed. "All right. Your daughter has done nothing but disgrace this family since the day she was born."

"What's so disgraceful about being in love?" Marie asked, lowering her voice. "She's in love with him, you know."

"Love?" he scoffed. "You're as foolish now as you were at nineteen. Love is nothing to compared to family...Brandon knows that as well as I. This infatuation your daughter has will end in nothing other than more disgrace. And after last night—"

"Stop it!" Marie cried. "You know nothing about love! You know nothing about what one will give up or endure for another person. You've never loved anyone but yourself or anything but your own power!"

"That's enough!" He made a slicing gesture with his hand. "You should've done what I asked. A good daughter would have gone away... we have family in France who would have taken care of—"

"Gone away and come back nine months later with no baby," she mocked, her face white with rage. "Didn't you also suggest seeing one of those 'special' doctors?"

"And if you'd done what I'd asked, the family would have been spared *years* of embarrassment. Of course, if you'd acted with the class and breeding of a Delacroix, you never would have become involved with that trash in the first place."

"Get out!" She pointed toward the door, her hand trembling so badly her entire arm shook. "You're in my house, and I won't allow you speak to me this way. Now, get out!"

Veronique stepped into the doorway, her head spinning with what she'd overheard. So her grandfather wished she'd never been born. His dislike had always been obvious, but to hear the truth so plainly was like a knife in her chest.

But what of her mother? Veronique gazed at her mother's white, pained face, and her eyes filled with tears. Until today, she hadn't realized just how much her mother *did* love her, how much she'd given up to have her. Veronique squared her shoulders and stepped forward. "You heard her," she said quietly. "Get out."

Veronique thought she saw surprise flicker in his eyes when he saw her. That look was instantaneously replaced by nonchalance. He shrugged, then collected his hat and jacket. "You'll regret this, Marie Elizabeth," he said, then added, "Remember, family is everything." A moment later he was gone.

"Maman, are you all right?" Veronique crossed to the other woman and put an arm around her. Her mother's shoulders quaked under her arm, and Veronique hugged her more tightly.

"I wish you hadn't heard that," Marie murmured, her words as unsteady as her body.

Pain arced through Veronique again as her grandfather's words filled her head. She pushed them determinedly away. "It's okay."

"No...no, it's not." Marie's voice strengthened as she spoke. "No child should hear that they weren't wanted."

"But *you* wanted me," Veronique said softly. "Listening to Grandfather made me realize how much."

Marie stepped out of the comforting circle of Veronique's arm. "Outwardly you've always been so brave...so sure of yourself. But deep down I know how you hurt. I feel responsible."

"You've had nothing to do with other people's cruelty, Maman."

Marie laughed; the sound filled with remorse. "If I'd been a braver woman, a stronger woman, I would have taken you and left New Orleans." She lowered her eyes. "But I'm not brave, Veronique. I'm not strong. I've only stood up to your grandfather twice in my life, and today was one of those times." She lifted her eyes. "Earlier, you looked so happy, but now..." She reached up and touched Veronique's cheek. "Now you're pale and look sad. It's all my fault."

"No," Veronique murmured, "not your fault. Earlier I was just being foolish."

"Don't say that. You weren't being foolish." Marie grabbed Veronique's hands and took a deep breath. "I should have done this long ago. It's time to tell you about your father."

Veronique's breath caught and hope clutched at her heart. She'd waited twenty-eight years to hear her mother say those words and... and now she was almost afraid to learn the truth. "Why?" she asked hoarsely. "Why now?"

Marie looked away. "Because I want you to know about love...you've known so little of it in your life. Because now you have a chance at happiness. Sometimes you only get one, and I don't want you to give up on it." Her voice cracked, and she crossed to the fountain and stared down at the sparkling water. When she spoke again, her tone was even but laced with regret. "I met your father in the spring. The azaleas were in full bloom; the breeze off the Gulf was warm and sweet. I was on my way to afternoon Mass, hurrying because I'd lingered too long in a dress shop; he was feeding the pigeons the last of his sandwich. I ran into him and dropped my packages. When he stooped to help me retrieve them, our hands touched, our eyes met. I'll never forget the sensation—it was like falling off a cliff, but instead of speeding toward the earth, I floated." Even now, thirty years later, she blushed at the memory. "I never made it to Mass—we spent that afternoon together and every other minute we could."

Marie turned away from the window to face Veronique. "There weren't as many minutes as we would have liked . . . we had to hide our love from my parents. You see, he had nothing, and . . ." Her words trailed off, and she began wringing her hands.

"And what, Maman?" Veronique urged.

"His name was David Goldstein," she finished quietly.

Veronique stared blankly at her mother a moment, then comprehension dawned. "He was Jewish," she murmured, sinking onto the couch. There was a whole culture, rich with tradition, that she hadn't even known belonged to her.

"I didn't care," Marie rushed on. "But I knew Father would be furious. David wanted to go to him, try to reason with him, but I begged him not to." Her eyes filled with tears. "Right after I found I was pregnant, Father discovered our secret."

"How?" Veronique felt her mother's pain and ached for her.

"I made the mistake of confiding in my best friend. She told her mother." Marie's shoulders drooped. "It was the beginning of the end."

"Oh, Maman . . ."

Marie's smile was bittersweet as she recounted the past. "We had such fun together. Your father was full of energy and ideas. He made me laugh. And he was a gentle man, kind and good." She shook her head. "Sometimes when I allow myself to remember . . . I still can't believe he deserted me."

Tears sprang to Veronique's eyes; she blinked them away. "What happened?"

"I don't know. I've always suspected your grandfather had something to do with David leaving, but . . . I never had the courage to confront him." She laughed, the sound was brittle and filled with self-loathing. "But maybe that's just my fantasy, my way of lessening the pain."

"But maybe not," Veronique muttered. Knowing the depth of her grandfather's hatred of anyone unlike himself, she could imagine his rage at his daughter's involvement. She could also imagine the lengths he would have gone to break up the young lovers.

Marie continued as if Veronique hadn't spoken. "When I told David I was pregnant, he was delighted. He wanted us to marry. He said we'd run away if my father gave us trouble. He said he loved me and would move heaven and earth for us to be together. That was the last time I saw him. We had a date to meet at the Cathedral. He never—" The tears that threatened spilled over, rolling slowly down her cheeks.

"Oh, Maman." Veronique stood and crossed to her mother. She captured her hands and squeezed them. "I'm sorry to cause you more pain, but I..." Veronique drew in a deep breath. "What did he look like, Maman? What business was he in? Was he athletic? Artistic? I'm sorry, but I've waited so long to know."

"It's your right. I should have told you long ago...but I couldn't bring myself to...speak of him." Marie's lips thinned with determination. "Your father looked like you— tall and slim, moody brown eyes and thick dark hair. He was artistic—as you are—but not particularly athletic. He was Blake Rhodes's partner and—"

"What?" Veronique interrupted, surprised. "He was a partner in Rhodes?"

"Mmm. It was all very hush-hush. I don't think anyone knew but me and the store's attorney."

Veronique's brows drew together. "But why was it a secret? That doesn't make any sense."

Marie shrugged. "The store was David's idea; Blake put up all the capital. They made some agreement... something about using the Rhodes name exclusively."

"That's it? You don't know any other details?"

"No. Your father and I had precious few hours together, and when we did ... we didn't talk about business."

Veronique understood. She could picture the young lovers, heads bent together, laughing about their future, whispering their love and their plans. "What happened?"

"When David disappeared, I went to see Blake. He said David had come to him and asked if he would buy his half of the business. He said David had seemed desperate and ... Blake was very kind." Marie's voice broke, and she pressed her face into her hands.

Feeling her mother's despair and humiliation, Veronique wrapped her arms around her and held her while she wept.

The sun made its final dip in the west. Veronique didn't bother to turn on the lights in her apartment, but instead sat staring into the rapidly darkening room. It had been hours since she'd left her mother's house. And in that time she'd gone over what her mother had told her, again and again.

The more she'd thought about it, the more something didn't add up. She plucked at the sleeve of her nubby red sweater. Brandon had told her his father started Rhodes, that he'd originated it. Why wouldn't Brandon, the store's future successor, know about the partnership? It didn't make sense.

Unless ... something was crooked.

Veronique rubbed her temples. She had instincts about people, about situations, and this smelled dirty. But what could she do? Blake Rhodes was dead, her father was God only knew where and ... Her eyes narrowed. What had mother said? Only she, the principals and the store's attorney knew the truth.

That was it! All she had to do was talk to the lawyer. Who was he? She'd seen him a half dozen times at the store and had even been introduced once. She searched her memory.

Setton...Samuels...what was his name? With a small shake of her head, she jumped up and raced for the phone book.

Samuel, Scott...Sebastian. That was it! Without pausing for thought, she tore the page from the book, grabbed her purse and headed downstairs to hail a cab.

Twenty-five minutes later, the cab pulled up in front of a luxurious Tudor-style home in Old Metairie. She told the cabbie to wait until she was inside the house, then took a deep breath. She'd bluffed her way into pool halls underage, out of speeding tickets and into parties without invitations. Tonight she was going to try to bluff out the truth. Squaring her shoulders, she headed up the walk.

By the time Sebastian opened the door, Veronique had psyched herself up for the confrontation. Looking furious, she pushed past him into the house, then turned to face him. "I know all about it! You had better be a good lawyer, because—"

"Who are you? I'm calling the police."

Veronique waved toward the phone. "Go right ahead, Mr. Sebastian. When they get here, I'll explain all about Blake Rhodes and David Goldstein and your part in it."

The man stopped and turned. His eyes met hers, recognition flickered in them. "You're—"

"Veronique Delacroix," she inserted smoothly, lifting her chin in challenge.

"My God—"

"Bingo. Still want to call the police?"

"Why don't we go into my office?"

Veronique inclined her head, then followed him. It seemed she'd pushed the right buttons. It also seemed she'd been right—something here stunk.

The lawyer closed the door behind them, then turned toward her. "I don't know what you've heard, but—"

"I've heard it all, Mr. Sebastian." She placed her fists on her hips. "I wonder what the state bar association will think of my little story? And I wonder what your other clients will think when it hits the paper? Interesting to speculate, isn't it?"

The man paled. "Look, Blake and Goldstein's relationship ended years before I became the store's attorney. Apparently my predecessor was in on it, but—"

"How convenient," she interrupted, sarcastically. "You expect me to believe you had nothing to do with any of if?"

"Of course. Why should I lie?"

Veronique's eyes flicked over him. "You have plenty of reasons to lie." When he didn't respond, she took a stab in the dark. "Knowing that a man cheated his partner sounds like a pretty good 'why.'" Veronique knew she'd hit a nerve when the gleam of sweat appeared on his brow. In a nervous gesture, he pulled out a handkerchief and wiped it.

"Okay, I knew about it. But as I said a moment ago, *after* the fact. Five years had passed when Blake came to me, concerned that Goldstein would show up and demand his share. When we discovered he'd been killed in an accident—"

Veronique felt as if he'd kicked her. Any fantasies she'd harbored of finding her father had just been destroyed. She held her breath to keep from making a sound of pain.

"—Believe me, Ms. Delacroix, had I been Blake Rhodes's attorney at the time, I would have advised him against his actions. And if he'd insisted, I would have resigned as counsel. But coming in after the fact, my legal responsibilities were limited."

Time for another stab, she thought, noting his returning confidence. "What about Jerome Delacroix's part in it?" she demanded.

When his face slackened with surprise, Veronique thought she'd missed her mark and would have to backpedal, and quickly, or the man would begin to suspect how much she really knew.

"That was a family matter. Again, I would have advised Blake against getting involved—especially in a matter as serious as framing someone for a crime they didn't commit. As for your grandfather, I had no part in that, nor was the store involved.''

Veronique felt sick. She tried to keep the revulsion and pain from showing on her face. Poor Maman, she thought. She'd been right, David wouldn't have left her; it was her own father and Blake Rhodes's machinations that had taken her love. Veronique wondered how was she going to tell her. And what of Brandon? How would he handle the news that his father was a crook? When the lawyer cleared his throat, she glanced back at him.

"As I'm sure Brandon told you," he said, his tone as smooth as silk, "we are prepared to make you a substantial offer.''

Veronique blanched, suddenly feeling as if all her supports had been yanked away. It couldn't be true, she thought frantically. Brandon couldn't have known and not told her.

"Or did Brandon already present you with a settlement? If so...'' His voice trailed off. "Are you all right?''

She wasn't. Pain was swift, debilitating. Her knees began to buckle, and she looked around for a chair. Finding one, she sank into it. Brandon had lied to her, tricked her.

"My dear, can I do anything?''

"Yes,'' Veronique said stiffly. "Call me a cab.''

The light was on above Brandon's door; his Porsche was parked in the driveway. Veronique stared at the elegant old house for long moments before paying the cabbie and heading up the walk. She was breathless with anger. The blood drummed in her head, and tension tightened across her temple. Sucking in a sharp breath, she rang the bell.

Within moments Brandon answered the door. He was dressed casually; he looked relaxed, even sleepy. Veronique swore under her breath as he smiled at her. The curving of his lips was slow, sexy and full of promise. The promise of tenderness and passion. Memories flooded her senses: the way those lips had tasted against hers, the way he'd aroused her with the simplest touch, the gentlest caress...the way he'd felt inside her.

Cursing again, she pushed away the memories. Her grandfather was right. To a man like Brandon, power and position came first. She'd been a fool.

"May I come in?"

He seemed surprised at her icy tone, but he moved aside. She brushed past him, stepping into a large, open foyer. From what she could see of the house, it was appointed with fine antiques, contemporary art and priceless rugs. Of course, she thought bitterly, nothing but the best for Brandon Rhodes.

"When you and your mother do lunch, you really do lunch. I didn't think you were coming."

She swung back toward Brandon. As she stared at him, rage and disillusionment welled in her chest until she thought she might burst with it.

Brandon tilted his head. "Are you all right?"

She lifted her chin and narrowed her eyes. "I had an interesting afternoon."

"Oh?" He shoved his hands into his pockets.

"Mmm, I'd even call it enlightening." She crossed to a small, delicately painted abstract. "O'Keeffe?"

The question wasn't meant to be answered, but he did anyway. "Yeah."

She swung back around, pinning him with her furious gaze. The game of cat and mouse was over. "I know who my father was...I know *what* your father was."

Brandon paled. "How?" he asked, his voice hoarse.

Pain ripped through her. Even though she'd known the truth, she'd prayed it wasn't true, and prayed it was a mistake. And he hadn't even tried to deny it. "Does it matter?" She hated the disillusionment in her voice.

"No one knew but—"

"But you and Sebastian," Veronique finished, her hands curling into fists. "You made one mistake: you didn't take into account what my mother knew. And she knew enough to raise my suspicions."

"So, you went to see Sebastian."

His voice was even, his gaze steady. She wanted to hit him. The need to do violence was so strong it took her breath away. Her fingers flexed as she glared at him. "For a man in his position, he was easily duped."

"I was going to tell you."

That he would try to backtrack, make excuses, hurt more than the truth. "When?" she cried, "In a year? In ten?"

"It's not like that, Veronique," he said softly, soothingly. "I was going to tell you tonight."

"Oh, right." She laughed without humor. "How convenient for you. And how stupid do you think I am?"

He crossed to her and grabbed her hands. His voice suddenly hummed with sincerity. "What can I say to convince you?"

"Words mean nothing." She jerked her hands from his. "How long have you known?"

"Not long. Since right after my father's funeral."

She lifted a trembling hand to her lips as she remembered all the times she'd shared her fears, her vulnerabilities with him, and all those times he'd known about her father.

"I discovered a safety deposit box," he continued. "In it were some documents that clearly indicated what had happened. Then I went to see Sebastian. I have the documents here if you'd like to see them. There's a newspaper clipping... your father's picture."

A picture of her father. Twenty-eight years of wondering, fantasizing was about to come to an end. And she was scared witless. "Yes," she whispered, her palms wet, her chest tight.

He lead her to his study, then went around the massive desk and took a large envelope from one of the drawers. "You might want to sit down," he said softly.

She did, then held out her hand. Her fingers shook as she opened the flap and pulled out the bundle of documents. Taking a deep breath, she began to read.

Ten minutes later Veronique looked up at him with anguished eyes. "What else do you know?"

"Everything."

"Tell me," she murmured, her eyes lowering once again to the picture of her father.

When he'd finished, Veronique carefully refolded the photograph and tucked it into her bag. A single tear rolled down her cheek, and she brushed it away. Her throat ached with the force of holding the rest of the tears back, but she refused to let them loose in front of Brandon. Mustering all her strength of will, she said, "I still can't believe you kept this from me."

"I didn't tell you right away because I was trying to decide what to do." He dragged his hands through his hair. "Believe me, when I found out what my father had done, I was appalled, disillusioned."

"But instead of telling me—"

"At first, my only thought was of protecting myself and the business. I didn't know how you'd react, what you might do. I thought I needed time to get to know you . . . to gauge your reaction to the news. But, as time passed I became afraid that you'd misinterpret my silence. More than anything in the world, Veronique, I didn't want to hurt you." His voice lowered. "I didn't want to lose you."

"Pretty words, Brandon." Her eyes raked accusingly over him. "You should have been a writer . . . or an actor."

"What can I do to convince you?" He held a hand out to her in supplication. "Tonight, I'd planned to offer you a settlement—"

She was out of her seat in a flash. "God, you make me sick! You and your kind think money is the answer for everything. Keep your dirty money! I wouldn't want to become what you are or what your father was." She stood, squared her shoulders and lifted her chin. Feeling as if she were being split in two, she said, "Goodbye, Brandon."

Eleven

Suck eggs, Rhodes," Veronique muttered, crumpling the interoffice memo and stuffing it in her pocket. Except for a few brief encounters, she'd managed to avoid Brandon for the last two weeks, and she wasn't about to let his scrawled "see me today" change that. She wandered to the coffeepot and poured a cup, then looked around the room. Where was Chip this morning?

Shrugging, Veronique crossed to the table and plopped down onto a chair. With a sigh, she leaned her head back and closed her eyes. She could honestly say the last two weeks had been the worst of her life. Telling her mother what she'd learned had been wrenching. Her beautiful mother had crumpled before her eyes, and all she'd been able to do was hold her and try to comfort her.

"Oh, Maman," Veronique had murmured, stroking her hair. "I'm so sorry."

"N-no." Maire lifted her tear-streaked face. "I finally know the truth. David loved me. You can't imagine what it feels like to know he didn't—" Her voice caught on a sob.

Veronique reached around them for the box of tissues. She handed her mother one.

After she'd blown her nose, Marie continued. "For years I've felt like a failure—to my family, as a woman. And so guilty...." She drew in a deep, shuddering breath. "Your grandfather...all these years he made me feel like I wasn't a good daughter. He encouraged my guilt...and now I learn *he's* the one who should be ashamed."

Two days after that conversation her mother had stopped by. Veronique smiled as she remembered. Marie had looked happier, more at peace, than she'd ever seen her. She'd breathlessly confided that she'd just paid a visit to her father and soundly told him off!

Veronique's smile faded. What about her own feelings? she wondered, rubbing her aching temples. Dealing with her mother, Brandon and her own turmoil over what she'd learned had left her emotionally drained. And Brandon hadn't made it any easier. He wouldn't take no for an answer. He'd called every day; she'd hung up on him each time. He'd sent her flowers; she'd sent them back. He'd tried to corner her at the store; she'd outmaneuvered him.

But every time he pressed, it was harder to act cool and unaffected. Veronique balled her hands into fists. She would never let him see how he'd destroyed her. *Never.*

She sighed. All the resolutions in the world weren't going to change the fact that she still loved him, that she ached for him. Veronique laughed without humor. Her only crime had been forgetting the lessons of her past and falling for him. For such a little crime, she was paying an exacting price.

Whenever she thought of it, she felt like a fool. How could she have hoped for a future with Brandon? How could she have allowed herself to be swept away by passion? By romance? She'd let stories of lovers like Courtland and Alfonsi cloud her judgment. She shook her head as unwanted tears filled her eyes. Brandon wasn't Courtland; giving everything away for love was as farfetched as the possibility that he would ever have married her. If only she could—

"Veronique!" Chip burst through the metal double doors at the back of the display department. "You're not going to believe this!"

Veronique's head snapped up, and she quickly swiped at her damp cheeks with the heels of her hands. When she was certain he wouldn't suspect she'd been crying, she turned toward him. Her eyebrows rose at his animated expression. Chip was the most unemotional person she knew. "What's going on?"

"This—" He gestured grandly. "Come on, guys."

Veronique's mouth dropped as three delivery men started wheeling in crates. There were at least a dozen of them; they ranged in size from three to six feet.

"I got a call from receiving this morning and . . . take a look." Chip held out the packing slip.

She stood, crossed to him and took the piece of paper from his hand. She scanned the list in amazement. The shipment was from The Display Warehouse, and these crates represented only the tip of the iceberg. "There must be some mistake, I didn't order these." All three delivery men stopped working and stared at her. They didn't look happy.

Her eyes lowered once again to the list. There were new mannequins, the two neon fixtures she'd wanted for juniors and young men's, faux boulders—in fact, this list was almost a duplicate of the one she'd handed Brandon weeks ago. Including the automated mannequin.

She tried to suppress her growing excitement. It might be a mistake. They may have . . . what? "I'll need to authorize this purchase before signing for it."

The phone call took only a minute. Purchasing verified the shipment; the delivery men breathed a sigh of relief and finished hauling in the crates. Chip began prying open the containers and pulling out the straw packing, exclaiming as the contents of each were revealed.

Veronique just stared at the slip of paper in her hands. Brandon had done this. There was no one else who had the authority to spend this kind of money, nor had she shown anyone else her proposal. The props were a peace offering; he was betting they would work where flowers had failed.

He was wrong. Veronique's eyes narrowed, and her fingers tightened on the packing slip. If he'd ordered the props out of a real belief in her ideas and judgment, she would have been touched. But he'd done it out of guilt; he was attempting to *buy* her forgiveness, and she couldn't be bought.

If she accepted the shipment, he would think he'd won. She caught her lower lip between her teeth. She couldn't send it back—it was too important to her, she wanted the props too badly. And Brandon knew it.

Anger flared, and she came to a decision. She was going to accept the shipment but make it clear that was *all* she was accepting. "Chip, hold down the fort. I'll be right back."

Five minutes later Veronique stepped into Brandon's reception area. "Hi, Maggie. Is Brandon in?" Veronique forced a cheerful smile.

"Yes, but..." The woman's voice trailed off, and she sneaked a peek at his closed door from the corners of her eyes. "He's been in such a foul mood lately. I don't know what's wrong, but he's been acting like a bear with a thorn in his paw. He might not see you without an appointment."

So, Brandon had been in a foul mood, Veronique thought, her lips curving. It served him right. "No problem," she said easily, and pulled the crumpled memo from her pocket. "He told me to stop by sometime today."

Maggie looked relieved. "I'll tell him you're here."

Moments later the receptionist told her to go in. Veronique's mouth went dry when she saw him. He was wearing a charcoal-gray suit; his tie was loosened, his hair rumpled. And he looked tired. His eyes were shadowed, and the tiny lines radiating from them seemed more deeply etched than before. She caught the warmth a moment before it blossomed in her chest, and she hardened her heart. It served him right; she hoped he never slept again.

Squaring her shoulders, she tossed the packing slip onto his desk. "I got your message. All of them." Before he could speak, she added, "And I want to make something perfectly clear—I'm accepting the props only because I know they're right for the store. Not because I forgive you. Not as a peace offering." She swept her hair away from her face. "There will be no peace. Is that clear?"

"Veronique—"

"Is that clear?" she demanded again, shoving her shaking hands into her trouser pockets. He hadn't shaved, she thought, then silently swore as she remembered how his rough chin had aroused the delicate skin of her abdomen.

He dragged a hand through his thick, dark hair. "Sit down...we need to talk."

His voice was soft, coaxing. She steeled herself against its effect on her. "You had the chance to talk before...you wasted it."

When he saw her turn to leave, he was up and around the desk in a flash. He grabbed her by the elbows. "We *need* to talk," he repeated. His gaze, of its own accord, lowered to her mouth and lingered there.

Her heart thundered in her chest. He wanted her. She read it in his hungry gaze, felt it in his hands as they held her. And, God help her, she wanted him. What had happened to her cool determination? she asked herself. What had happened to her unflappable calm? Her racing pulse made determination laughable; her hot cheeks and trembling hands made calm absurd.

"You're not being reasonable," he said softly. "Let's talk this over. There's no sense in—"

Reasonable? she thought furiously. "If you don't take your hands off me—right now—I'm going to scream. Remember, I don't care about my reputation."

Her voice had a deadly edge, and Brandon drew in a deep breath. She wasn't kidding, but he wasn't about to let her go now. "You're not playing fair, Veronique."

"Fair? Who was the one who kept secrets? Who was the one who poked and probed, the whole time knowing the truth...the whole time laughing behind my back? Don't talk to me about fair."

"I never laughed at you, Veronique." He slid his hands from her elbows to her shoulders. "I did what I thought I had to, but I hated it. I should have trusted you, I know that now. I'm sorry."

Her eyes flooded with tears; she blinked them away. She would not cry, she vowed, clinging to her composure. She would not let him see her pain. Taking a deep, steadying breath, she said icily, "This conversation is over."

"No." He pulled her toward him, stopping only when her breath mixed with his and the tips of her breasts barely brushed against his chest. "I was going to tell you, Veronique. What can I say to convince you of that?"

"Nothing." He looked as if he meant to kiss her, and she silently swore. If he did, she would melt against him. She should have known better than to come up here. Nothing had been solved; she'd only made the pain worse by proving to herself how much she still wanted him. Feeling exposed and foolish, she stepped away from his hands. "I guess we'll never know."

Brandon watched her walk out the door, a heavy ache in his chest. He missed her. What an understatement, he thought derisively. The truth was, every time she walked away from him, he felt as if he were dying inside. He'd never realized before how important one person could become to another. But then, he'd never shared himself and his life with anyone.

He'd been such a fool. What would she say if he told her he'd fallen in love with her? She would probably laugh in his face. And he wouldn't blame her if she did. He could see how he looked in her eyes—like the Blake Rhodeses and Jerome Delacroix of the world, power and money hungry, more concerned with position and portfolio than with other people or genuine emotion.

Maybe he had been like that once. Maybe that's why he'd been so unhappy. Veronique had changed all that—she'd changed his life. There had to be a way of convincing her that his motivations, if not completely honest, had been honorable.

He narrowed his eyes in consideration. The lines of communication had to be opened. Traditional gifts like flowers hadn't worked. Nor had the props or sincerity. How was he going to get her attention?

It would have to be something big, something public, flamboyant, he decided. It would have to be something that Veronique herself would do.

His eyes crinkled at the corners a moment before he laughed.

Veronique tossed aside her book in disgust. It had been a week since the initial shipment of props had arrived at the store. Since then two more shipments had been delivered; today she and Chip had placed the automated mannequin in the front window. The store was being transformed, and she'd been congratulated by countless persons—from buyers to clerks—on how great it looked. The response from customers had been excellent; the store had been busy, sales up.

Then why wasn't she happy? Why didn't she feel a glow of satisfaction at seeing her dreams come true? Because all of her dreams *weren't* coming true, she answered. Because as hard as she tried to push Brandon from her mind, he was all she could think about.

Apparently he'd taken her at her word; he hadn't tried to contact her since she'd confronted him about the props. There'd been no calls and no flowers...and she was glad. Really, she was. The corners of her mouth turned down in sarcasm. That's why she'd been unable to laugh with friends or sleep through the night. The truth was, there was a pain inside her middle that wouldn't go away, and she didn't know what to do.

There was a soft rapping on her front door, and grateful for the distraction, she sprang from the couch to answer it. Her lips curved into a welcoming smile when she saw her mother. "Maman, what a nice surprise. Come in."

"Hi, sweetie."

Veronique embraced her, pressing a kiss to her cheek. "You look great," she murmured, taking in the snappy pants outfit, flushed cheeks and sparkling eyes.

The flush deepened. "Do you really think so?" Marie looked down at her outfit in concern. "I don't feel quite right wearing slacks yet."

"You look great," Veronique repeated firmly. "Come on, I'll buy you a cup of coffee."

"Are you alone?" Marie asked, following Veronique, her gaze darting over the empty living room.

Veronique lifted her eyebrows in surprise. What an odd and unexpected question. "Is there some reason I shouldn't be?"

"I suppose not."

Her mother's response lacked conviction, and Veronique cut her a glance from the corners of her eyes. Could it be her mother was even redder? She took two cups from the cupboard, filled them, then handed one to Marie. "What brings you here tonight?"

"I would think you could guess, Veronique."

"Oh?" What was going on? Her mother looked like the proverbial cat with a canary. "You're being mysterious, Maman."

The other woman only shrugged and sipped her coffee.

Veronique tilted her head and tried again. "So tell me, what's new?"

Marie glanced down at her hands, then back to Veronique. "A man asked me for a date."

"A date," Veronique echoed, surprised. "What did you say?"

Marie's expression was at once flustered and determined. "I said yes. His name is John Billings, and he's a plastic surgeon. I met him at the Courtland's high tea."

At the mention of the Courtland Hotel, Veronique's heart leapt to her throat, and she ignored the desire to cry. "That's great news, Maman! I'm so happy for you."

"But that isn't why I'm here, and you know it," Marie said, lashes lowering coquettishly. "I brought you this." She pulled a lavishly wrapped box out of her shopping bag and handed it to Veronique.

"For me?" Veronique asked, pleased. She took the box from her mother's hands, ripped the paper away and tossed aside the lid. Nestled inside layers of delicate tissue was a white silk negligee. With a squeal of delight, Veronique pulled it from the box and held it up. It was simply styled of elegant unadorned silk, cut low in front and in at the waist. "Oh, Maman, I love it."

"I wanted you to have something really special..." Her tone was suddenly husky with tears, quivering with reproach. "I can't believe you didn't tell me, your *own* mother."

"Tell you what?" Veronique asked, stroking the shiny fabric.

"About your betrothal to Brandon Rhodes. Really, that I should have to read it in the paper like everyone else! I couldn't believe—"

"My what!" Veronique's eyes flew to her mother's in shock.

"Your betrothal to..." Marie's voice trailed off. "Are you all right?"

She wasn't. It was as if all the blood had drained from her body. She felt numb. After a moment, Veronique carefully refolded the negligee. When she trusted her voice, she asked, "Who told you this?"

"Why, I read it in Sissy's column... Isn't it... true?"

"No, Maman, it's not," Veronique said woodenly as pain ripped through her. The thing she wanted most but couldn't have was being cruelly dangled in front of her. When all she wanted was to forget Brandon, pretend that nothing had ever been between them, her name was being linked with his in the most intimate way.

Marriage. She squeezed her eyes shut for a moment, then looked at her mother. "You're absolutely sure?"

"Yes. It was in this morning's paper. Do you have—"

Veronique didn't give her time to finish the question. She raced to the living room. She hadn't read it, but she hadn't tossed it out, either. It still lay folded on the coffee table. She yanked the rubber band off and tore through the paper until she found Sissy's column. There it was, in black and white.

New Orleans Bachelor of the Year to wed.
Brandon Rhodes, owner of Rhódes and this year's *Crescent City Magazine* Bachelor of the Year, pri-

vately confided his engagement to Veronique Delacroix today. The news came as quite a shock, even though the couple's names had been linked on numerous occasions over the past months. Needless to say, the unexpected and unconventional coupling will set many tongues wagging and many an unmarried lady weeping...

Veronique crushed the newsprint under her fingers. Why was he doing this? Why was he publicly humiliating her? Did he think he could just continue the game he'd started so many weeks ago? Did he think that this time, like last, she would take the dare and play along?

"Veronique, can I do anything?"

She turned her eyes to her mother's concerned face and forced a weak smile. "Could I borrow your car?"

In the time it took to drop her mother off at home then drive to Brandon's house, Veronique had worked herself into an awesome temper. Fuming, she slammed the door of her mother's Mercedes and stalked up the brick walk. So, an engagement between them was a big joke? He was so much better than her that a marriage between them was an amusing game? Well...then...he was the one who wasn't good enough for her! She could outclass any of his snobby friends or family. Ignoring the bell and knocker, she pounded on the door with her fist.

When he opened it, she swept past him. Once inside, she whirled around. "Not this time, Brandon Rhodes!"

She'd read the paper, Brandon thought. And she was spitting mad. He said a silent prayer even as he cooly raised his eyebrows. "Not this time *what*, Veronique?"

She pushed her hair back from her face and pinned him with her furious gaze. "This time I turn down the dare. There will be no game and no peace. I want you to leave me alone."

"No." He took a step toward her, almost laughing out loud when her mouth dropped.

The man was impossible! "What do you mean, 'no'?"

He took another step, liking that he'd surprised her, liking even better that she was off balance. He would need every edge he could get. "Just what it sounds like—no, I won't leave you alone." Another step, and he was inches from her. "What are you going to do about it?"

Veronique lifted her chin. How dare he challenge her! "Slap an injunction on you, that's what. Or file a harrassment suit. I won't allow you to tell Sissy lies."

He tipped his head, his grin wicked. "I thought you didn't care about your reputation?"

"This is different," she spat. "And you know it."

"Yeah?" Catching her off guard, Brandon tumbled her into his arms. "Refresh my memory."

Veronique gasped and squirmed against his embrace. "Let me go... what are you doing?"

"What do you think?"

Her heart flew to her throat; she had difficulty talking around it. "I won't stand for this. You think I'm so crazy about you that you can treat me any way you want and I'll forgive you? Or so in love with you that you can deceive me and I'll still fall into your arms, no questions, no explanations? Well, Brandon Rhodes, you have a lot to learn about—"

"Well, *are* you?" he interrupted, trailing his lips across her jaw. "Crazy in love with me?"

Delicious sensations skated up her spine and teased every nerve ending. She steeled herself to remain stiff in his arms. It was one of the hardest things she'd ever done. Trying to summon her haughtiest tone, she said, "You are the most egotistical man... I can't believe I ever got involved with you... what a fool I was to..." She choked back a sigh as he caught her earlobe between his teeth and nipped, then soothed the spot with his tongue. "Why are you doing this?" she cried, frustrated by his unwillingness to reason, pushed to the breaking point by his touch and her own need. "Why won't you leave me alone?"

"Because I can't." He caught her lips in a quick kiss, retreated, then caught them again. "In case you haven't noticed, I haven't been able to leave you alone since our first meeting." Her throat was warm and white. He tasted it with the tip of his tongue. "You feel the same, Veronique. I can tell by the way you melt against me... by the way you shudder under my touch. We're meant to be in one another's arms."

Pain was a living thing inside her. Everything he said was true, but it wasn't enough. Not for her. She needed more—she needed forever. He loosened his arms and she stepped out of them. Eyes swimming with tears, she turned away, not wanting him to see them.

She might as well end it now, Veronique thought, looking at the floor. She would tell him how she felt, talk about marriage, then he would leave her alone. She wouldn't have to worry about Brandon Rhodes's attentions ever again. "What about love?" she asked, her voice husky with tears. "What about total commitment? I didn't have a real family as a child... I want one now. An affair—even a passionately caring one—isn't enough."

Brandon came up behind her and placed his hands on her shoulders. They were tight with tension, and he began gently massaging them. "I planted the story about our engagement with Sissy because I knew you wouldn't let it pass. I had to talk to you...I couldn't believe what a fool I'd been, and—" he took a deep breath "—when I gave Sissy the story, I'd hoped we wouldn't be submitting a retraction."

Veronique turned. "What are you saying?"

He cupped her face in his hands and tenderly stroked her damp cheeks. "I'm asking you to marry me.... I'm saying . . ." His voice was suddenly rough with emotion. "I'm saying I love you."

Joy burgeoned in her chest. Brandon loved her! He wanted to marry— As suddenly as it had bloomed, the joy withered and died. Veronique almost cried out loud. The seed of doubt had been planted—she didn't wholly believe the thing she wanted most in the world to hear. Did he really love her, or was he protecting himself and the store from future lawsuits?

He saw the denial race into her eyes, and panic came upon him so quickly he was breathless with it. "There's more, I—"

"What about trust, Brandon?" she interrupted, her voice high and thin. "I want you, but I'd never be able to trust you. Even if I said I believed you were going to tell me about my father and Rhodes, there would always be some doubt. It would stand forever between us. I wouldn't be able to live with myself and my doubts, and you would become bitter because you would know that I didn't wholly believe in you."

Brandon pulled her back into his arms. She was stiff and unyielding; he held her anyway. "I had Sebastian draw up some papers," he said softly. "I asked myself how I could prove to you that I'd meant to tell you, that I was the honorable man my father was not. I realized there was only one way. You can have it all, Veronique. Because all I want is you."

Veronique stared at him as if he'd lost his mind. "You'd give the store away? Why? That's the most illogical thing I've ever heard. If anything, I'm only entitled to half. And even then—"

He placed a finger against her lips. "This isn't about logic, Veronique. It's about love. You make me happy, you make me whole. I want to marry you. . . . I want us to be together. And I want you to know I'll do anything to make that happen.''

Hope ballooned inside her. He was offering to give her everything to prove his love. That which she said he would never do, he was doing. The things she'd thought most important to him—wealth, position, power—he was willing to live without to live with her.

Her heart began drumming in her chest. All those question he'd asked her about her father, about her feelings . . . of course! He *had* been planning to tell her! She'd been too blinded by pride and past hurts to see the truth. And because of that, she could have lost him.

Reaching up, she cupped his face with trembling hands. Her lips curved into a tender smile. ''How did you know I'd believe you?''

Relief washed over him. For the first time since losing her, he felt as if tomorrow would be filled with more than time. Brandon's smile mirrored hers. ''I didn't, but I had to take a chance.''

''I like a man who takes chances,'' she murmured, moving provocatively against him.

''Yeah?'' His arms tightened around her.

''Ummm . . .'' She caught his lower lip between her teeth and gently tugged. ''But more, I like a man who takes liberties.''

Brandon laughed against her lips. ''Where have I heard that before?''

''Probably some hussy.'' Veronique began unbuttoning his shirt. When she reached his waistband, she tugged the shirt out and pushed it off his shoulders. ''Probably some woman who did incredible things to your body.'' She ran her palms over his naked back and her tongue along his shoulders.

''I think you're right.'' He slipped his hands under her loose-fitting cotton shirt and stroked her satiny skin. ''She was the most beautiful, most exciting woman I'd ever known." With one quick jerk, he had the shirt over her head. "I fell in love with her," he murmured, lowering his lips to hers. "There'll never be anyone else."

His mouth met hers—it was like coming home. Tremors raced along her spine; she sighed and deepened her kiss. He was all the adventure, all the fun and excitement she would ever need. Catching his tongue, she melted against him. "Make love to me, Brandon."

"Yes," he murmured. Sweeping her into his arms, he carried her up the stairs. "But the slate floor's too cold... too hard."

"I don't care." Threading her fingers through his hair, she smiled up at him.

"But I do." His bedroom was cool and dark. He laid her on the bed, then sank down next to her. With a tenderness he wouldn't have thought himself capable of, he gazed down at her. "I never want you to be uncomfortable... or unhappy... or lonely."

"How could I be if I'm with you?" She held out her arms. "Come here..."

Soon words were no longer possible as they moved together, unable to deny or prolong their passion. As she reached the peak and crested it, Veronique cried out her love. The sweetest moment of her life came when he whispered it back.

Long, lazy moments passed. Flesh cooled, hearts slowed. Veronique sighed and stretched. "Brandon?"

He trailed a finger over her damp belly. "Hmm?"

"What possessed you to plant that first blurb in Sissy's column? How did you know I'd take the bait?"

"Has lovemaking made you light-headed?" he teased. "I didn't plant that, you did."

Veronique lifted on her elbow to stare down at him. "Are you saying that you didn't give Sissy that story?" When he nodded, she frowned thoughtfully. "If you didn't and I didn't, *who* did?"

Brandon laughed and rolled her on top of him. "Who cares?"

She laughed with him and nuzzled his throat. "Well, I for one would like to say thank you. Without that blurb, we might not be here."

Brandon tightened his arms possessively around her. "You're right. Thanks, whoever," he whispered a second before his lips covered hers.

Epilogue

Sunlight streamed through the cathedral's stained-glass windows, dappling the interior in warm, colored light. The strains of jazz drifted in from outside the church's massive doors and mixed with the murmured vows of the man and woman at the altar.

The old man stood alone at the back of the church. The light blue suit he wore looked as fresh and crisp as it had weeks ago. He looked down at the fine worsted and smiled—it was the suit he would have chosen to wear to Brandon's wedding.

Things were as they should be, he thought with satisfaction. Marie Delacroix believed in both dreaming and love again. Brandon was happy, in love, having it all. He would never be like his father was—consumed by regret, lonely and bitter.

And Veronique. His eyes filled with tears as he stared at the woman responsible for Brandon's bright future, the woman who would make Brandon himself a father. She was strong, giving, filled with life. And now she had what was rightfully hers—half of Rhodes and her proper place in New Orleans society. He laughed to himself. Not that she cared about either.

As the couple's lips met, his heart swelled with joy for Marie, Brandon and Veronique—but mostly for himself. For the first time in years he felt as if he could go on without feeling strangled by "if onlys," without constantly looking over his shoulder and wishing for another chance. He felt he could be at peace.

He'd started something he could be proud of, something good. Something that would bring new life into the world.

The couple turned, and laughing, started down the aisle. Yes, indeed, the man decided, watching as Brandon stopped in the middle of the church to pull his bride back into his arms for a long leisurely kiss, some things worked out after all. With a whispered goodbye, he turned and walked through the cathedral's massive, closed doors.

*   *   *   *   *

MAURA SEGER

A compelling trilogy stretching from the Civil War to the twentieth century and chronicling the lives of three passionate women.

SARAH is the story of an independent woman's fight for freedom during the Civil War and her love for the one man who kindles her pride and passion.	$3.95	☐
ELIZABETH, set in the aftermath of the Civil War, is the tale of a divided nation's struggle to become one and two tempestuous hearts striving for everlasting love.	$3.95	☐
CATHERINE chronicles the love story of an upper-class beauty and a handsome Irishman in turn-of-the-century Boston.	$3.95 U.S.	☐
	$4.50 Cdn.	☐

Total Amount	$	_____
Plus 75¢ Postage		.75
Payment enclosed	$	_____

Please send a check or money order payable to Worldwide Library.

In the U.S.A.	In Canada
Worldwide Library	Worldwide Library
901 Fuhrmann Blvd.	P.O. Box 609
Box 1325	Fort Erie, Ontario
Buffalo, NY 14269-1325	L2A 5X3

Please Print

Name: _____

Address: _____

City: _____

State/Prov: _____

Zip/Postal Code: _____

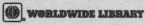 **WORLDWIDE LIBRARY**

SEG-3